My Husband's Wild Desires

by John Tobias

A SAMUEL FRENCH ACTING EDITION

NEW YORK HOLLYWOOD LONDON TORONTO

SAMUELFRENCH.COM

ISBN 978-0-573-69872-9   Printed in U.S.A.   #15177

MUSIC USE NOTE

Licensees are solely responsible for obtaining formal written permission from copyright owners to use copyrighted music in the performance of this play and are strongly cautioned to do so. If no such permission is obtained by the licensee, then the licensee must use only original music that the licensee owns and controls. Licensees are solely responsible and liable for all music clearances and shall indemnify the copyright owners of the play and their licensing agent, Samuel French, Inc., against any costs, expenses, losses and liabilities arising from the use of music by licensees.

IMPORTANT BILLING AND CREDIT REQUIREMENTS

All producers of *MY HUSBAND'S WILD DESIRES must* give credit to the Author of the Play in all programs distributed in connection with performances of the Play, and in all instances in which the title of the Play appears for the purposes of advertising, publicizing or otherwise exploiting the Play and/or a production. The name of the Author *must* appear on a separate line on which no other name appears, immediately following the title and *must* appear in size of type not less than fifty percent of the size of the title type.

An early version of **MY HUSBAND'S WILD DESIRES** was produced at the Studio Arena Theatre in Buffalo, New York. The current version has been produced by leading theatres in Paris, Montreal, Capetown, Copenhagen, Rio de Janeiro, Warsaw (three years at Teatr Bajka), Stockholm, Beunos Aires, Antwerp, Bucharest, and most recently Tokyo (2009) and Moscow (2010). The hit of the season at Tokyo's Le Theatre Glinza, **DESIRES** starred Japan's leading actress. Tetsuko Kuroyanagi, officially honored as a "National Treasure" by the Emperor and Diet of Japan.

"Dear John, thank you again for your beautiful play. I have never done such a funny role as Mrs. Greffin before. We all talk about sex, but such an elegant play! There is nothing sorid. All that exist is an explosion of laughter!" – Tetsuko Kuroyanagi

CHARACTERS

(in order of appearance)

BURGLAR – skinny, nervous-looking, around fifty.

MRS. GRIFFIN – an elegantly attractive woman in her forties with the calmly self-assured bearing of someone who probably did her pre-teen shopping at Bergdorff-Goodman's.

CONNELLY – a super in his late-forties whose body has the look of a once-burly frame softened by immersion in oceans of beer. His broad face wears the serenity appropriate to one who has come to accept life in terms of a little something on the side or under the table.

MR. GRIFFIN – beetle-browed, square-jawed, the perfect picture of a successful middle-aged business executive.

LOUISE – Mrs. Griffin's sister. Thin, sad-eyed, pushing forty, given to collapsing helplessly a lot.

SETTING

The action of the play takes place in a contemporary upper East Side Manhattan apartment.

TIME

Act One:
The Griffins' apartment, a spring afternoon.

Act Two:
Shortly after.

ACT ONE

Spring, the present; upscale Manhattan apartment.

The curtain rises on the bedroom – and part of the living room – of the Griffins' apartment. The living room extends off stage right where the unseen front door and entrance hall are. The bedroom dominates. The room, contains a double-bed, a vanity table, a chair and a small occasional table, which holds a telephone, a humidor and an ashtray, plus two closets.

Furnishings suggest upper middle class comfort. Furniture is period. Tasteful, unobtrusive paintings.

A stage left window, framed by open drapes, reveals afternoon view of surrounding rooftops.

A couple of seconds after the curtain rises, we hear front door buzzer from offstage right. After a long buzz there is a pause, then an even longer buzz, as though someone wants to be sure nobody's home. After a second pause, we hear the sound of someone fumbling at the lock, then a click and the sound of the door being opened and closed.

A skinny, nervous-looking **BURGLAR**, *neatly dressed but wearing gloves and crepe soled shoes, enters the living room. He gives the room a quick, jumpy appraisal, picks up an ornament, makes a face, puts it back.*

He drifts toward the bedroom, peeks nervously inside, enters, and starts rummaging through some drawers. He comes up with a watch. It strikes him as singularly unimpressive, but he pockets it anyway. He rummages some more. His hand encounters an object that evidently surprises him. He takes it out – we can't see what it is and puts it in his breast pocket. He goes to closet 1, opens it, and grins happily if twitchily at the sight of some expensive furs, then freezes in sudden panic at the sound of someone entering the apartment. He looks about wildly, just manages to get inside and close the door as **MRS. GRIFFIN** *sweeps into the living room.*

She is an elegantly attractive woman in her forties with a calmly self-assured manner. She wears an expensive-looking hostess gown.

MRS. GRIFFIN. *(very noblesse oblige)* Thank you for coming so promptly, Mr. Connelly…

(**CONNELLY**, *a man in his late-forties wearing a blue shirt with "Super" lettered on it and carrying a metal tool box, follows her into the room. His body has the look of a once-burly frame softened by long-term immersion in oceans of beer and his broad red face wears an expression of grave serenity appropriate to one who has come to accept life in terms of a little something on the side, a little something under the table.)*

CONNELLY. *(pompously)* Well, it wasn't easy, Mrs. Griffin. 11D's faucet is dripping, 3C has got a broken sash, and I should be checkin' on the painters in 5F – if you don't stay on their tails, they're liable to take all day.

MRS. GRIFFIN. Well, I do appreciate it.

CONNELLY. Glad to hear that. Some tenants it just don't pay to put yourself out for – especially some of the types they've been renting to lately. You break your back trying to solve their problem, and they don't even have the common decency to show a little gratitude. *(shakes his head more in sadness than in anger)* Present company excepted, of course. When you and Mr. Griffin moved in, I said to myself, "These are high-class people–they know how to *appreciate*."

MRS. GRIFFIN. Thank you.

CONNELLY. Don't mention it. Now then! *(briskly)* The bedroom radiator, you say?

MRS. GRIFFIN. *(preceding him into bedroom)* Yes.

CONNELLY. *(entering bedroom)* Well, we'll see, we'll see.

(He goes up to the radiator, tentatively places his hand on it and frowns abstractly, like a doctor taking a temperature. After a few seconds, he announces:)

It's cold.

MRS. GRIFFIN. I know.

CONNELLY. Official confirmation, Mrs. Griffin... *(drawing notebook and pencil from breast pocket)* A matter of notations to be made and procedures to be followed.

MRS. GRIFFIN. I understand..

CONNELLY. *(reciting ponderously as he writes in notebook)* "14C: Heat...lack of *(puts notebook away)* First the diagnosis, then the cure. Now then! *(puts down tool-case, opens it, thoughtfully considers its contents, takes out a hammer)* First we test for simple blockage.

MRS. GRIFFIN. Blockage?

CONNELLY. An obstruction in the passageway, *(leans over radiator)* caused by accumulated sediment...corrosion...With all the chemical pollution that's around *(raises the hammer)* it's no wonder we're in trouble... *(bangs the radiator)* But this should do the trick... *(bang, bang, bang)* assuming our problem is blockage. *(straightens up, eyes radiator unhappily)* There are, of course, other possible factors to consider: air pockets, faulty pressure gauges, defective fuel pumps –

MRS. GRIFFIN. I didn't realize it was so complicated.

CONNELLY. New developments in the field every day, Mrs. Griffin: It's a strain just keeping up. But we'll sort it out. *(walks frowningly around the radiator)* A matter of making observations, considering alternatives, applying a logical –

MRS. GRIFFIN. Would you like a drink?

CONNELLY. Huh?

MRS. GRIFFIN. *(serenely sympathetic)* You've been working so hard...

CONNELLY. Well... *(lowers hammer)* I *have* been on the go all day.

MRS. GRIFFIN. Trying to solve other people's problems... always thinking of others...

CONNELLY. *(struck by her insight)* That's the God's own truth. You're an understanding woman, Mrs. Griffin.

MRS. GRIFFIN. Thank you. Scotch?' Bourbon? Vodka?

CONNELLY. Well, if you insist... *(indicating a large drink with his fingers)* A little Scotch on the rocks would be nice.

MRS. GRIFFIN. *(exiting to living room)* I'll be right back.

CONNELLY. *(eyeing her retreating figure)* Fine, fine...and we'll solve your little problem, Don't worry.

MRS. GRIFFIN. I'm not worried. *(at liquor cabinet in drawing room)* I know I'm in expert hands.

CONNELLY. *(alone in bedroom, complacently)* Well, I may not have a college degree... *(spots humidor on table, drifts towards it)* but sixteen years of practical experience, handling all sorts of equipment, emergencies, people–

MRS. GRIFFIN. *(mixing drinks in living room)* That's something you can't get from books.

CONNELLY. Exactly. *(takes lid off humidor)* Not that a lot of them students want to learn, anyway... *(takes out cigar, crackles it thoughtfully under his nose)* Too busy tattooing themselves and taking drugs. *(shakes his head sadly)* What's the world coming to? *(stuffs a couple of cigars in his pocket)* Where will it all end?

MRS. GRIFFIN. *(appraising her image coolly in the mirror)* Try not to lose heart, Mr. Connelly. *(arranges hair loosely, seductively)* There are millions of decent, concerned citizens like yourself holding the line...

CONNELLY. *(replacing humidor lid)* Each and every night, the wife and I get down on our four knees and thank God for the likes of you and Mr. Griffin. Especially when you see some of the lot they're letting in the building lately... *(wandering back to radiator)* Girls with earrings on their tongues or weirder places...Guys with technicolor hair...

*(As **CONNELLY** shakes his head, **MRS. GRIFFIN**, eyeing reflection with serene composure, arranges herself to reveal some bosom)*

You don't know what it means to me to see Mr. Griffin stepping briskly out of the elevator every morning....

(gazes reverently out over the audience as **MRS. GRIFFIN** *after a final critical appraisal, picks up the drinks and sweeps towards the bedroom)*

wearing a sharply pressed suit and a striped tie, swinging his attache case – it makes me feel maybe there's some hope after all.

MRS. GRIFFIN. *(coming to him)* We must all live in hope, Mr. Connelly.

CONNELLY. I guess so. *(taking preferred drink automatically)* Well, here's to – *(He becomes aware of her altered appearance.)* to....

MRS. GRIFFIN. *(glowing serenely)* To *warmth.*

(clinks glasses with the temporarily immobilized **CONNELLY,** *who is staring at her cleavage)*

CONNELLY. Warmth. Yes. Of course. I uh... *(takes a flustered gulp of drink)* I see what you mean. It's a matter of...uh...temperature control... *(wrenching his eyes to the radiator)* exploring all possible factors, checking, testing...*(fumbles with radiator knobs)* eliminating each – Just a minute! *(stares at knob)* I think I see your problem – *(turns knob)* Yes, sir, that's it, all right – *(announces triumphantly)* The radiator was turned off!

MRS. GRIFFIN. It was?

CONNELLY. *(with great satisfaction)* I knew we'd sort it out sooner or later...

(gives knob a final, triumphant twist as **MRS. GRIFFIN** *says:)*

MRS. GRIFFIN. How could I be so careless?

CONNELLY. A lot of people get confused. *(takes out notebook, crosses off radiator entry)* Anti-clockwise is *ON* you see, and clockwise is off.

MRS. GRIFFIN. *(thoughtfully)* I don't think it was just confusion.

CONNELLY. Oh?

MRS. GRIFFIN. I think… Yes – *(nods with growing conviction)* I'm sure of it now…I turned it off from an unconscious need to talk to you in private – so that you could advise me on another deeper, more important problem…

(**CONNELLY** *automatically turns a notebook page, poises his pencil.*)

No notations, please. This is of a confidential, personal nature.

CONNELLY. Well, I… *(uncertainly puts his notebook and pencil away)* I'm not sure I'm equipped to –

MRS. GRIFFIN. *(earnestly)* Oh, but you are, Mr. Connelly. *(sits on bed)* Sit down, please.

(He hesitates, then sits awkwardly on a chair across from her, takes up his drink. She eyes him thoughtfully for a second)

Is it the way you like it?

CONNELLY. Huh?

MRS. GRIFFIN. Your drink.

CONNELLY. Oh, yeah. Fine.

(He takes a swallow; she watches.)

Very smooth.

MRS. GRIFFIN. I knew you'd take your whiskey straight…

CONNELLY. You did?

MRS. GRIFFIN. No frills, no compromises: meeting life head on with a simple, direct strength and honesty.

CONNELLY. Well… *(unable to find anything here to argue with)* It's the way I was brought up, I suppose. I've always tried to –

MRS. GRIFFIN. Look at me, Mr. Connelly!

(She leans forward, gravely earnest, causing the front of her gown to pop open still further.)

What do you see?

(He stares glassy-eyed, at her now generously exposed breasts as she continues thoughtfully.)

I think I can guess: you see a woman with a luxurious apartment, a successful husband, social standing…In short, a woman who has everything –

(**CONNELLY** *is still mesmerized by her bosom.*)

Am I right, Mr. Connelly?

CONNELLY. (*Wrenching his eyes up to her face – he hasn't heard a word she said.*) Huh?

MRS. GRIFFIN. And yet – I tell you this in strictest confidence – it all seems empty, hollow, meaningless… *Why?* Can you answer me that?

(*He opens his mouth.*)

I'll tell you why.

(*He closes his mouth.*)

Because I lack the one thing a woman needs to be really happy. Do you know what that is?

CONNELLY. Well… (*uncomfortably*) There are various factors to be –

MRS. GRIFFIN. *Warmth,* Mr. Connelly; that's what a woman needs. The kind that *doesn't* come out of a radiator…

(*puts her hand on his as he takes a nervous gulp of whiskey*)

Simple, direct, honest human –

CONNELLY. (*putting drink down and rising nervously*) I think I'd better be –

MRS. GRIFFIN. (*rising with him*) What's the matter?

CONNELLY. (*heading for tool-case*) The painters… (*picks up tool-case*) I really ought to be checking on –

MRS. GRIFFIN. Did you think – my God, you did – (*turns her back on him*) I can see it in your eyes…

CONNELLY. What?

MRS. GRIFFIN. Just because I spoke of warmth… (*distractedly*) you thought I was being disloyal to my husband…

CONNELLY. No, no, I –

MRS. GRIFFIN. What will he say when I tell him?

CONNELLY. (*alarmed*) Jesus! Don't tell that! (*comes up to her*) What do you want to tell him that for?

MRS. GRIFFIN. It was in your eyes…

CONNELLY. It was not! The thought never entered my mind!

(She turns and regards him tremulously.)

MRS. GRIFFIN. It didn't?

CONNELLY. I swear to God!

MRS. GRIFFIN. I…I suppose I might believe you if only *(shy, vulnerable)* you didn't rush off so abruptly…

CONNELLY. Well…

MRS. GRIFFIN. *(more in sorrow than in anger)* Not that my husband would really care one way or another…

CONNELLY. Oh?

MRS. GRIFFIN. Even if he were here instead of in Spokane.

CONNELLY. *(blinking)* Spokane.

MRS. GRIFFIN. *(sadly)* Three thousand miles away…

CONNELLY. I suppose…*(putting down tool-case)* a few more minutes….

MRS. GRIFFIN. *(handing him his drink)* Thank you.

CONNELLY. *(taking it)* Don't mention it.

MRS. GRIFFIN. You see, a sense of loyalty has always been extremely important to me.

CONNELLY. I've never doubted it.

MRS. GRIFFIN. Even though there's *(shrugs helplessly)* such a distance between my husband and myself.

CONNELLY. *(nodding)* Three thousand –

MRS. GRIFFIN. When he's home, it's no different.

CONNELLY. Oh?

MRS. GRIFFIN. I – *(hesitates, turns away)* I shouldn't be troubling you with all this.

CONNELLY. That's all right.

MRS. GRIFFIN. It's just… *(turns to him with a trusting, vulnerable expression)* I think he cares more about his ball bearings than he does about me….

CONNELLY. Ball bearings?

MRS. GRIFFIN. His company makes them.

CONNELLY. Oh.

MRS. GRIFFIN. *(sadly)* He's always going off alone on sales trips – Detroit, Chicago, Spokane….

CONNELLY. I'm sorry to hear that.

MRS. GRIFFIN. Even when he's here, he's not really… *(hesitates)* I mean, imagine – just for a moment, Mr. Connelly – that you are my husband and you've just come home in the evening and…*(takes a shy step towards him)* here I am.

    (CONNELLY *takes a nervous gulp of whiskey as she looks up at him, lips half-parted, eyes melting.)*

Would you sit down and start working on some sales report?

CONNELLY. Well…uh…I don't think so…*(takes another gulp)* Not right away…

MRS. GRIFFIN. No. Not you… *(eyes him with glowing admiration)* You haven't cut yourself off from feeling… You don't spend your days lifting telephones, dictating memos, eating shrimp cocktails on jet planes… You're a natural man, working with your hands, sweating, cursing, drinking your whiskey straight, quick to laughter, to anger, to love – I don't mean to embarrass you –

CONNELLY. That's all right.

MRS. GRIFFIN. And I'm not blaming my husband…

CONNELLY. No, no.

MRS. GRIFFIN. It's not his fault that civilization has deprived him of your primitive spontaneity and strength and gusto, your huge lust for – *(catches herself, as though suddenly remembering something)* Forgive me – I have no right to speak to you like this.

CONNELLY. Why not?

MRS. GRIFFIN. You're a married man.

CONNELLY. *(impatiently)* Don't worry about it!

    (She eyes him inquisitively.)

I mean… *(awkwardly)* Mrs. Connelly is a fine woman… good with the kids and the house and like that…only…

MRS. GRIFFIN. She doesn't appreciate you?

CONNELLY. She prefers TV.

MRS. GRIFFIN. I knew it!

CONNELLY. You did?

MRS. GRIFFIN. *(staring at him glowingly)* I sensed from the first that you and I shared the same need for warmth… *(takes a step towards him)* …the same deeply spiritual commitment to honest human emotion.

CONNELLY. *(mesmerized, as she looks up meltingly into his eyes)* Yeah…

MRS. GRIFFIN. We can't go on like this…

CONNELLY. No…

MRS. GRIFFIN. Tension…frustration…eating us up…tearing us apart…

CONNELLY. Jesus…

MRS. GRIFFIN.…leading to constant bickering between husband and wife…

CONNELLY. *(nodding feverishly)* Bickering…yes, bickering!

MRS. GRIFFIN. Ending in divorce, heartache, ruined lives – is that what we want?

CONNELLY. No!

(He stares at her, all fired up as she says quietly, solemnly.)

MRS. GRIFFIN. Then we must do everything we can to relieve that tension…that frustration…Fortunately… *(wandering over to the window)* it's perfectly reasonable that you pop in from time to time to fix something…

CONNELLY. *(nodding)* There's always work to be done.

MRS. GRIFFIN. Remember, Mr. Connelly… *(draws the drapes)* we're doing this not only for ourselves… *(comes back to him, glowing serenely)* but for the *sake* of our *marriages*.

CONNELLY. Right.

MRS. GRIFFIN. Another drink?

*(**CONNELLY** starts to hand her his glass, then hesitates. There is a long pause.)*

CONNELLY. Spokane?

MRS. GRIFFIN. *(taking his glass)* Spokane.

(She moves towards the living room, turns back at the bedroom door, smiles warmly.)

I won't be a minute…

(He nods dazedly, eyes her disappearing figure, then turns, begins to move about the room with increasing self-assurance, a hint of a swagger, as though a primitive, earthy strength and vitality is beginning to assert itself…

He goes to the humidor, grabs a fistful of cigars this time, sticks them in his pocket, swaggers on, catches sight of himself in a full-length mirror, sucks his belly in, frowns masterfully at his reflection.

While he is doing this, **MRS. GRIFFIN**, *after pouring a drink, is arranging herself even more seductively in front of the living room mirror…*

CONNELLY *leaves the bedroom mirror and moves about with an increasingly proprietary air. He glances into the bathroom, heads past closet 1 to the bed, tests the softness of the bed with his hand, nods approvingly…then he opens the door of closet 2 more or less in passing, glances carelessly inside – and is momentarily paralyzed by what he sees.*

Inside the closet is a tall, middle-aged **MAN**, *seated in a chair, leaning forward in an attitude which suggests he has been peering through the keyhole. This is* **MR. GRIFFIN**, *balding, square-jawed – the perfect picture of a successful business executive, except for the fact that he is presently attired in a woman's cocktail dress and high-heeled shoes.*

As the stupefied **CONNELLY** *gapes at him,* **MR. GRIFFIN**, *with an annoyed expression, reaches for the inner door handle, and slams the door in his face.*

CONNELLY *blinks dazedly at the closed door, backs slowly away, turns, grabs up his tool-case and heads into the living room, to be blocked by* **MRS. GRIFFIN** *coming toward him with a drink.)*

MRS. GRIFFIN. Why, Mr. Connelly – what's wrong?

CONNELLY. *(flustered)* I…the painters…*(tries to get past her)* I really –

MRS. GRIFFIN. *(blocking him)* What is it?

(He stares at her numbly, then blurts out:)

CONNELLY. Your husband's not in Spokane – *(jerks his thumb towards the bedroom)* He's in the closet.

MRS. GRIFFIN. *(slight pause)* Oh, dear… *(reproachfully)* You peeked.

*(**CONNELLY** blinks at her.)*

CONNELLY. You mean – you *knew* he was in the closet?

MRS. GRIFFIN. It's nothing to concern yourself a –

CONNELLY. But he's – he's wearin' some kind of a… *(vague gestures)* Well, he's *not* dressed for the office!

MRS. GRIFFIN. *(reasonably)* He's not *in* the office.

*(**CONNELLY** stares at her blankly, begins to nod his head.)*

CONNELLY. Right.

*(He edges nervously away. In the bedroom we see the **BURGLAR** poke his head cautiously out of closet 1.)*

MRS. GRIFFIN. There's really a very simple explanation, if you'll –

CONNELLY. *(edging around her)* 3C. 9E.

MRS. GRIFFIN. *(puzzled)* I don't –

CONNELLY. *Psychiatrists.*

*(The **BURGLAR** sees the outline of the fire escape outside the bathroom window and hesitates, glancing nervously from the window to the argument in the living room as **CONNELLY** bolts around **MRS. GRIFFIN** and she grabs his arm.)*

MRS. GRIFFIN. Wait –

CONNELLY. *(struggling to get free)* Let go!

MRS. GRIFFIN. I can explain –

CONNELLY. I *don't* – *(wrenching free)* want to hear it…

(He heads for the hall exit as the **BURGLAR** *finally gets up his courage and tiptoes out of the closet with the furs, and* **MRS. GRIFFIN***, with a resigned shrug, draws a deep breath and screams after* **CONNELLY***:)*

MRS. GRIFFIN. *Rape!*

*(***CONNELLY** *and the* **BURGLAR** *jump like startled rabbits and the* **BURGLAR** *bolts back into the closet.)*

CONNELLY. Jesus –

MRS. GRIFFIN. Help!! Rape!!

CONNELLY. *(rushing back to her)* Don't do that!

MRS. GRIFFIN. *(firmly) Rape.*

CONNELLY. Please – the neighbors… *(glances nervously toward the bedroom)* Your husband…

MRS. GRIFFIN. He won't mind. *(as* **CONNELLY** *stares at her numbly)* He'll simply testify to the police that you rushed out of here – it's really very annoying, the way you're always rushing out of here – when he arrived home unexpectedly and surprised you attempting to ravish me –

CONNELLY. *(shaking his head in feeble protest)* No…

MRS. GRIFFIN. You prefer "rape"? Maybe you're right; it's a pithier word.

CONNELLY. I didn't. You – you wouldn't…

MRS. GRIFFIN. We don't want to, but…*(shrugs helplessly)* we simply can't have you running out on us now after all this time and –

CONNELLY. I'll tell them it's a lie! *(backs away)* Nobody'll believe you…

MRS. GRIFFIN. Really, Mr. Connelly – who would *you* believe? A highly respected executive – dressed for the office, of course – and his socially prominent wife…or you?

*(***CONNELLY** *looks a little sick as she continues thoughtfully.)*

Especially when I tell them how you forced your way in here to fix a radiator which obviously doesn't need to be fixed…and show them how you tore my gown with your clumsy, pawing, bestial advances…

(with a tinge of regret, to the increasingly unhappy-look-ing **CONNELLY***)*

MRS. GRIFFIN. *(cont.)* It's a designer original, but one must make – why, Mr. Connelly, what's the matter?

CONNELLY. I don't feel very well...

MRS. GRIFFIN. *(compassionately)* Oh, I *am* sorry – I didn't mean to upset you...you'd better sit down...

(The shaky **CONNELLY** *lets her conduct him to an easy chair.)*

There now...

(He lowers himself unsteadily into the chair.)

It's silly for two people who have so much in common to squabble like this.

(She hands **CONNELLY** *his drink; he takes it like an automaton, swallows.)*

Feeling better?

CONNELLY. *(weakly)* You – you wouldn't really...say those things about me, would you?

MRS. GRIFFIN. Not if you'll stop this foolishness and let me clarify the situation for you.... *(gently reproving)* It's your own fault, you know – if you hadn't peeked, it wouldn't be necessary.

CONNELLY. *(as his eyes wander uneasily toward the bedroom)* I'm sorry...

MRS. GRIFFIN. Let's just try to be honest and above-board with each other from now on; for without trust –

CONNELLY. Is your husband gonna *stay* in the closet?

MRS. GRIFFIN. *(reassuringly)* He's quite comfortable, really; it's air conditioned.

*(***CONNELLY*** *doesn't appear too happy to hear this as* **MRS. GRIFFIN** *says:)*

Well, now...how shall I begin? *(wanders about pensively)* Who can say when two people begin to drift apart...

when long silences replace the eager sharing of thought and emotion… *(shakes her head sadly)* I don't know exactly when it began. I only know that for some time now, my husband has found it increasingly difficult to – *(frowns, flutters her hand vertically in the air)* What is that expression?

CONNELLY. *(eyeing her hand)* Get it up?

MRS. GRIFFIN. *(with dignity)* Thank you. *(shyly)* I suppose we seem hopelessly old-fashioned to you, Mr. Connelly… but Mr. Griffin and I don't believe in taking marriage lightly, as so many young people appear to do today. *(reflectively)* We've put a lot of years into ours – years which have brought us many joys, including such dividends as a son at Princeton, a daughter at Vassar, and a vacation home in South Hampton. Still, Mr. Griffin's concern over the growing infrequency of his get-it-up-ability *has* been putting an increasing strain on our marriage.

(The living room phone rings.)

Of course, we tried Viagra. But my husband was one of the allergic ones.

(Second ring. She frowns at living room phone on top of answering machine.)

I thought I put the answering machine on.

(A third ring. She heads for the phone.)

I'll be right back.

(CONNELLY *sits clutching his drink, eyeing her uncertainly as she picks up the phone.)*

MRS. GRIFFIN. Yes, hello? Oh, Louise, can I call you back, I – *(listens, then impatiently)* Louise, I'm in the middle of – just can't – *(trying to stem a torrent of words)* I'm sorry, Louise, not *now* – I'm in the middle of an important – no, you *can't* come over here now – *absolutely not* – I'll call you.

(hangs up, puts answering machine on, returns to **CONNELLY**, *shaking her head)*

MRS. GRIFFIN. That was my sister. She always thinks her problems take precedence. But we've *all* got problems, *(eyes* **CONNELLY** *gravely)* don't we, Mr. Connelly?

CONNELLY. *(heartfelt)* Oh, yeah…

MRS. GRIFFIN. We must each solve our own. Mr. Griffin and I, for example, have always tried to maintain a high performance level in all areas. We've never seen ourselves as falling short. But… *(falters, as anxiety creeps into her voice)* according to the latest statistics on marital norms, we simply weren't performing up to our expected frequency level. Can you imagine how upset this made us both feel? *(slight frown)* It *did* occur to me that my husband might be… *(vertical hand flutter)* for someone else. When I questioned him on this point, he confessed to me that he *had* attempted to test his performance potential at a ball-bearing convention in Minneapolis with the same result. *(turning to* **CONNELLY***)* We tried everything, Mr. Connelly, even psychotherapy; but all my husband found himself able to talk about was the effects of the recession on the stability of the stock market. And then, one day, a book caught Mr. Griffin's eye in a shop window: *(pauses, then, as if sharing a wondrous discovery)* LIVE YOUR FANTASY: A HANDBOOK TO HEALTH AND HAPPINESS by Dr. Leopold Baumgartner. Are you familiar with him?

*(***CONNELLY*** shakes his head.)*

(pause) A great man. *(moves off again)* My husband felt impelled to buy that book. As he started to read it, he was immediately struck by Dr Baumgartner's lucidity, his compassion, his deep insight into the human condition…He turned the pages with a sense of mounting excitement and revelation, unable to put the book down…

(stops) That night, Mr. Griffin suddenly switched off the news… *(looks out wide-eyed, remembering)* I sensed a new-found assurance, a quiet self-confidence in his manner as he told me he was positive he would be able to – *(vertical hand flutter)* if I wouldn't mind being ravished by a hairy brute while he watched from the closet in drag…

(She confesses to **CONNELLY**, *whose eyes have become rather glazed.)*

Frankly, I was a bit put off at first – until, at my husband's urging, I began to read LIVE YOUR FANTASY myself. *(moves about with growing excitement)* Soon, I, too, was under the spell of Dr. Baumgartner's common-sense approach to the human condition. He teaches us to accept our complexity, to take pride and joy in the richness of our inner lives…I began to feel what Dr. Baumgartner calls the "trapdoor to our unconscious" start to open – a long-buried truth rose to the surface, burst upon me like a shower of light… *(wonderingly)* Something in me had always *wanted* to be ravished by a hairy brute! *(to* **CONNELLY**, *eyes glowing)* Can you imagine how I felt at that moment? To be able to tell my husband – we share the same wishes! We want the same things! The only obstacle to a happy marriage could finally be removed, thanks to Dr. Baumgartner…*(looks fondly down at him)* and *you*…

CONNELLY. Can I please go now?

MRS. GRIFFIN. Of course not; *you're* the hairy brute. You're not exactly what I had in mind, but there are certain –

CONNELLY. You mean… *(pushes himself out of the chair)* You expect me to – *us* to – with *him* in the *closet?*

MRS. GRIFFIN. *(reassuringly)* He may come out when he feels more comfortable with you; but since this is the first time –

(She breaks off as **CONNELLY**, *shaking his head, begins to back towards the offstage hall door.)*

Oh, dear, you're not going to start that again.

CONNELLY. *(backing away)* I'm getting out of here...

MRS. GRIFFIN. We simply can't permit you to –

CONNELLY. *(disappearing from view as he heads for hall door)* I don't care what you tell people...Sixteen years I've been here...

MRS. GRIFFIN. Don't open that door –

CONNELLY. I've got a reputation...

MRS. GRIFFIN. As a Peeping Tom?

(There is a long pause. **CONNELLY** *reappears, his expression uneasy)*

CONNELLY. What do you mean?

MRS. GRIFFIN. Oh, come now, Mr. Connelly; we both know your fondness for crouching on fire escapes...

CONNELLY. *(after a pause)* Not...crouching exactly – I wouldn't call it crouching...

MRS. GRIFFIN. Oh?

CONNELLY. More like – making observations on the area for prowlers and burglars...yeah... *(nods judiciously) making observations,* that's what *I'd* call it.

MRS. GRIFFIN. *(pleasantly)* I've noticed how you always seem to be making observations through the drapes when I'm taking my bath...

*(***CONNELLY*** *blinks unhappily.)*

I must say you have remarkable powers of concentration... *(comes toward him)* My husband was able to take some excellent pictures of you from the roof without distracting you in the least.

CONNELLY. *(anxiously, as she holds up a plastic packet of photos)* Pictures?

MRS. GRIFFIN. *(letting a whole accordion strip of photos unfold and dangle from her hand)* I think they're quite good, really... *(as* **CONNELLY** *numbly stares at the pictures)* Notice the bulging eyes, the slack mouth – one can almost hear you breathing. You're a very heavy breather, you know.

CONNELLY. It's a sinus condition.

MRS. GRIFFIN. Care to have a closer look?

(**CONNELLY** *shakes his head morosely and she puts the photos away, saying*)

I don't want you to think we hold it against you – your being a Peeping Tom, I mean.

CONNELLY. You don't?

MRS. GRIFFIN. Actually…

(*She takes the numb* **CONNELLY**'s *arm and draws him back towards the centre of the living room.*)

I can't help but be flattered to think that you would go to all that trouble to express your admiration –

CONNELLY. (*stopping*) If you really feel that way –

MRS. GRIFFIN. *Unfortunately,* most people would tend to react somewhat differently if they saw these pictures… (*shakes her head sadly at the increasingly trapped-looking* **CONNELLY**) People lack an understanding heart… except for a few rare individuals like myself, my husband and you… (*eyes him warmly*) You can see why you're such a perfect choice. We know we can depend on your discretion–(*takes his arm again, draws him in the direction of the bedroom*) just as you can depend on ours if you co-operate…

CONNELLY. (*hanging back*) I – I just don't think I can handle it…

MRS. GRIFFIN. (*encouragingly*) Of course you can! Just think – no more fire escapes, no more worshipping me from afar – the initiative you've shown is finally being rewarded… (*frowns at the increasingly trapped-looking* **CONNELLY**) unless you no longer look upon me as a reward. I'd hate to think you've transferred your allegiance to some other bathroom window.

CONNELLY. That's not it – it's… (*looking uneasily toward bedroom*) Mr. Griffin…

MRS. GRIFFIN. (*reassuringly*) He's a hundred percent behind you!

CONNELLY. That's what makes me nervous – – him behind me in a woman's dress...

MRS. GRIFFIN. *(stiffly)* I can assure you – my husband is completely normal.

CONNELLY. *(looking far from convinced)* Then what's he doing dressed up like a woman?

MRS. GRIFFIN. *(with the cheerful patience of a teacher with a somewhat retarded child)* He's simply practicing compensatory role-reversal.

CONNELLY. *(blankly)* Oh?

MRS. GRIFFIN. That's what Dr. Baumgartner calls it. You see – all day long my husband has to play an aggressive, super-masculine role – or his competitors would eat him alive...Can you imagine what that does to a person? To constantly have to dominate other people... *(moving about, reflectively)* make them dance to your tune...go out of their way to serve you... *(beginning to like the sound of this)* anticipate your needs, make your happiness their first concern, do what you *tell* them to do without argument – *(stops herself with an effort)* The point is, we all need a change of pace from time to time – surely you can understand that.

CONNELLY. *(cautiously)* I suppose.

MRS. GRIFFIN. *(triumphantly)* Well, then! *(taking his arm again)* This is simply *his* change of *pace!* Anyway... *(gently shepherding him toward the bedroom)* you needn't have anything to do with him. Once you've helped him get it up by ravishing me, you can leave, and he'll take over for the ravishment climax.

CONNELLY. How's he gonna manage that? I mean – if he thinks he's a woman –

MRS. GRIFFIN. He thinks he's part lesbian.

CONNELLY. *(stopping in his track)* I need a drink.

MRS. GRIFFIN. *(tugging him forward)* That's just stage fright.....

CONNELLY. *(desperately)* Listen –

MRS. GRIFFIN. What now?

CONNELLY. I'm really not very hairy...

MRS. GRIFFIN. Hairiness isn't essential – *(dragging him to bedroom threshold)* as long as you're lower class...

CONNELLY. *(resisting being dragged over threshold)* I can't – I want to go home – I –

MRS. GRIFFIN. *(sternly)* Mr. Connelly!

(He stares at her dazedly.)

How do you feel about America?

CONNELLY. *(automatically)* Love it or leave it.

MRS. GRIFFIN. Then – consider what my husband's balls mean to this country! *(catches herself at* **CONNELLY**'s *reaction to the word)* Bearings. Ball *bearings.* There's not a plane or ship or any piece of heavy machinery that can function without them – my husband's work is vital to the defense and economic well-being of the country you profess to love...unless... *(frowns at him)* you want to see him crack under pressure...unless you're some kind of subversive...

CONNELLY. *No, No.*

MRS. GRIFFIN. Well, then! This is your chance to not only help save a marriage – *(taking his tool-case from him and setting it firmly down)* but to *do* something for your country.

CONNELLY. But I – Oh, Jesus – can't I just have one drink?

MRS. GRIFFIN. Too much liquor – *(dragging him into bedroom)* lowers the sex drive. *(She positions him in the bedroom area more or less in front of closet 2.)* Try to stay in this general area; the view from the closet is rather limited.

(As she briskly sets about taking down the bed cover, he stares uncertainly at the closet, takes a step towards it, speaks nervously to the closed door.)

CONNELLY. Mr. Griffin? *(pause)* It's me – Connelly. I...uh... well, your wife has instructed me on what she says you want me to do...I just want to be dead sure – for the record, you know – that you really want me to do it – alright?

(He waits anxiously. There is no answer.)

MRS. GRIFFIN. *(finishing with bedspread)* He really prefers to remain incognito.

CONNELLY. Oh.

MRS. GRIFFIN. It's best to pretend he isn't there.

CONNELLY. Right. *(He turns back to the closet, nodding nervously.)* I understand, Mr. Griffin – I'm to pretend you're not there and go on about my business – OK?

(As CONNELLY *waits anxiously for an answer, his eyes on the closet door,* MRS. GRIFFIN *strips off her housecoat and throws it on the bed, revealing an under-costume of a black lace corselet over black bikini panties, black fishnet stockings and garters over her high heels.)*

(still nodding at the closed closet door; then, as though to reassure himself) OK.

MRS. GRIFFIN. Shall we begin?

*(*CONNELLY *turns – and stares, mouth open, at her new look. As he gapes at her, she backs away from him with an expression of shock, holds hands up in front of her vital parts, and whispers in exaggerated, virginal alarm.)*

Who are you…What do you want…

CONNELLY. *(bewildered)* Huh?

MRS. GRIFFIN. *(maintaining her "surprised" pose, but in a normal, somewhat impatient voice)* Please get in character, Mr. Connelly; we've started the *fantasy*.

CONNELLY. Oh.

MRS. GRIFFIN. *(coaching him)* You are a shambling, low-browed coal miner – *(frowns pensively)* Or better still – a brutish, thick-necked peasant on the eve of the French Revolution… *(pleased)* Yes…You once caught a glimpse of me – the wife of your arrogant master, the Marquis – when my carriage knocked you down as you staggered along the village street under a heavy load of faggots.

CONNELLY. *(uncertainly)* Faggots?

MRS. GRIFFIN. *(frowning impatiently)* Firewood, grain sacks – it doesn't really matter. The point is, you have known *lust* for my soft, white aristocratic body ever since, mixed, of course, with a thirst for revenge…And now you have surprised me alone and half-naked in my boudoir. I stand before you, trembling helplessly with fright as your tiny, red-rimmed eyes devour my half-naked body…A vein starts to throb in your forehead… your breathing becomes heavy, labored…

(frowns)

Your *breathinq* becomes *heavy, labored…*

(CONNELLY *nervously begins to pant.)*

A French *peasant,* Mr. Connelly – not a French *poodle.*

(CONNELLY *slows the panting down.)*

As you stare at me, my terrified helplessness only increases your lust…you take a step towards me…

(CONNELLY *is concentrating on panting.)*

Now, Mr Connelly.

(The panting **CONNELLY** *takes a step forward.)*

And another…

(He takes another step.)

And another…

(He takes another step, and she holds her hands up in a gesture of terrified supplication and whispers.)

Don't….

(CONNELLY *stops uncertainly. After a second,* **MRS. GRIFFIN** *lowers her hands)*

When I say *don't,* Mr. Connelly, you're not supposed to don't – you're supposed to *do.* Is that clear?

CONNELLY. *(completely befuddled)* Uh…

(The telephone rings – and he springs for it, grateful for the diversion, as she tries to stop him.)

MRS. GRIFFIN. Don't answer –

CONNELLY. *(into phone)* Griffin residence! *(listens as she frantically signals him to hang up)* …just a minute…I'll see. *(to* **MRS. GRIFFIN***, covering mouthpiece)* It's your husband's office.

MR. GRIFFIN. *(from closet)* I'm not here!

CONNELLY. *(dutifully, into phone)* He says he's not –

(stops confusedly, covers mouthpiece again, shrugs helplessly at **MRS. GRIFFIN***)*

I'm sorry.

*(***MRS. GRIFFIN***, looking daggers at him, takes the phone, regains her composure, and speaks in her coolly serene, gracious lady voice.)*

MRS. GRIFFIN. This is Mrs. Griffin…Oh, yes, Mr Gilbey… I'm terribly sorry, but my husband isn't feeling well and doesn't want to be…but he left strict orders that… Oh? Well, if you feel it's really that vital… *(to the closet)* It's Mr. Gilbey, dear. He says the pot's boiling over on the Argus machine tool account and he needs your thinking.

(After a second, we hear a voice mutter from the closet.)

MR. GRIFFIN. *Damn.*

(The closet door opens, and **MR. GRIFFIN** *marches sternly out, grabs the phone, sits down, adjusts his dress and barks into the receiver.)*

All right, Gilbey what's the flap?

(As he listens impatiently, he gropes around inside the humidor, then – without looking at him – snaps his fingers at **CONNELLY***.)*

CONNELLY. Huh? Oh… *(hastily hands a purloined cigar to* **MR. GRIFFIN***, who clamps it between his teeth and barks into the phone:)*

MR. GRIFFIN. We promised them delivery on the twenty-first, didn't we? Well, then! Tell them that's what the contract says and that's when they'll get the shipment – not a day sooner!

(pause; rotates the cigar) So they're pushing you. You can push back, can't you? What are you – *(angrily crosses his legs, pulls down his skirt)* some kind of sissy? *(pause)* All right – and don't bother me any more – you're supposed to be *handling* things! *(slams the receiver back on the hook, glowers at it)* Bunch of incompetents! *(flips the cigar into an ashtray, strides back to closet 2)* Sorry for the interruption *(opens closet door, steps inside)* Carry on!

*(He closes the door behind him. **CONNELLY** blinks at the closed door.)*

MRS. GRIFFIN. Mr. Connelly?

*(**CONNELLY** turns to her.)*

Let the answering service take it from on.

CONNELLY. Right.

(She resumes her living fantasy position.)

MRS. GRIFFIN. Let's take it from the top. Ready?

CONNELLY. I…I guess so.

MRS. GRIFFIN. *(making a pathetic effort to shield her vulnerable, nubile body)* Start the breathing…

*(**CONNELLY** half-heartedly obliges.)*

The lust rises in you like sap as you stare at my heaving bosom, my terrified, pleading expression You take a step towards me…

*(**CONNELLY** steps forward like a zombie.)*

I stand rooted to the spot like a bird hypnotized by a snake as you take another step…

(He does so.)

And another…Slowly, your thick, calloused fingers reach out toward me…*reach out toward me…*

(He reaches out awkwardly.)

My flesh shrinks back as they come closer and closer and I whisper in horror – *don't* –

*(**CONNELLY** appears unable to proceed any further.)*

MRS. GRIFFIN. *(cont.) Don't…Don't…(Her expression becomes a trifle grim.) Don't… (She breaks off.)* Mr. Connelly – I thought I told you –

CONNELLY. I'm sorry, It's just…The thing is…I'm used to… *(mimics her vertical hand flutter)* on the fire escape.

MRS. GRIFFIN. *(blankly)* Fire escape?

CONNELLY. *(judiciously)* Well, it don't have to be a fire escape, exactly…as long as I can be making observations on you from some kind of hiding place while you more or less – well, you know – get undressed, take a bath, any of those various activities.

MRS. GRIFFIN. *(unhappily)* Is it absolutely essential?

CONNELLY. It would start me off – get the old motor revved up.

MRS. GRIFFIN. *(putting on her dressing gown again, speaking to closet door)* Sorry for the delay, dear, but we do want to get him revved up.

MR. GRIFFIN. *(from closet)* I'm not here!

CONNELLY. *(heading for closet 1)* Just peel your things off at your normal rate of speed… *(reaches for closet doorknob)* I'll be making observations from –

MRS. GRIFFIN. *(as he starts to turn knob)* Not there – I don't want you breathing all over my furs!

(He releases the knob.)

Behind the window drapes.

CONNELLY. *(plodding over to the drapes)* Right.

*(He gets behind the drapes as **MRS. GRIFFIN** struggles back into her dressing gown. She goes over to her vanity table, across from the drapes.)*

MRS. GRIFFIN. All set?

CONNELLY. *(from behind the drapes)* Uh-huh.

MRS. GRIFFIN. *(resignedly, seating herself at the vanity)* Here I am, alone in my boudoir, preparing to go to bed…

*(She turns so the hidden **CONNELLY** can get a good view of her figure and loosens the bodice of her gown.)*

I do wish my husband, the marquis, was here. There have been reports of rebellious peasants running amok in the neighborhood...

(She begins to brush her hair, arching her back so that her bosom stands out provocatively.)

He has gone with the servants to investigate the rumors...

(Her exaggerated brush strokes cause her breasts to jiggle.)

leaving only Jacques, the swineherd, to protect me.

(As she continues to brush and jiggle, the drapes stir fitfully.)

He's a surly, hulking, brutish oaf – but he *is* strong... *(puts down hairbrush)* and regular beatings have taught him obedience...

(She pensively draws back her gown to reveal a stockinged thigh and the agitation behind the drapes increases as we hear the beginning of heavy breathing.)

Although, sometimes, there is an expression in his pig-like eyes *(shudders, stands up)* I mustn't think about that...*(moves about slowly, loosening her gown as the breathing gets heavier)* I mustn't feed my imagination with those stories of rampaging peasants murdering their masters... *(slips gown off her shoulder)* and violating their mistresses...

(The heavy breathing gets louder as she slips the gown off the other shoulder.)

I must have courage...*(continues the striptease as the drapes get more and more agitated)* and expose my soft white... *(lets the gown sink to the floor)* vulnerable body to the night –

(The revved-up **CONNELLY** *pushes through the drape.)*

Oh! Jacques!

(He stares at her, breathing heavily.)

Why are you looking at me like that?

(He advances, she backs terror-stricken, towards the bed.)

MRS. GRIFFIN. Please, Jacques…You're not going to…

(She retreats piteously to the head of the bed as the heavy-breathing **CONNELLY** *follows.)*

You…You wouldn't…

(As the heavy-breathing **CONNELLY** *reaches for her, she suddenly pulls a bullwhip from beneath the pillow.)*

Back, you insolent dog!

(She cracks the whip at him at him and the startled **CONNELLY** *leaps backward.)*

CONNELLY. Jesus –

MRS. GRIFFIN. *(advancing on him)* You dare to lay your filthy hands on a member of the nobility?

CONNELLY. *(confusedly)* But –

MRS. GRIFFIN. *(cracking the whip over his head)* Down on your knees!

(The terrified **CONNELLY** *drops to his knees.)*

Now crawl like the dog you are!

CONNELLY. *(nervously eyeing the whip)* Look out with that –

MRS. GRIFFIN. You heard me – *crawl!* *(cracking whip again)* *Crawl* I said!

*(***CONNELLY*** begins to laboriously crawl around the room as she follows, cracking the whip.)*

Crawl! I'll teach you your place! I'll teach you to aspire after your betters…

*(***CONNELLY*** disappears behind the bed.)*

MR. GRIFFIN. *(from Closet 2, testily)* Where is he? I can't see him.

MRS. GRIFFIN. He's crawling.

MR. GRIFFIN. Well, when is he going to get to the ravishing part?

MRS. GRIFFIN. *(as* **CONNELLY** *emerges wearily from the other side of the bed)* Be patient.

(**CONNELLY** *collapses and lies panting on the rug as* **MR. GRIFFIN** *says snappishly.*)

MR. GRIFFIN. I've been patient! Can't we get on with it, for God's sake?

(**MRS. GRIFFIN** *puts her foot on the collapsed* **CON-NELLY**'s *back and addresses the door politely but firmly.*)

MRS. GRIFFIN. First, I have to humiliate him to the point where, goaded beyond endurance, he tears the whip from my hand, rips off my clothes, picks me up bodily and flings me on the bed.

CONNELLY. *(panting)* I don't think I'm up to that…

MRS. GRIFFIN. *(prodding him with her foot)* Crawl!

(**CONNELLY** *begins to crawl.*)

MR. GRIFFIN. Look – *(opens door)* I want him to stop crawling and start ravishing! *(to* **CONNELLY***)* Get up!

(**CONNELLY** *starts to get up.*)

MRS. GRIFFIN. *(cracking her whip)* On your knees!

(**CONNELLY** *drops down again as she says reprovingly to her husband*)

I wish you wouldn't interfere.

MR. GRIFFIN. Interfere! *(steps out of closet)* This is my fantasy, isn't it? *(to* **CONNELLY***)* Get up!

MRS. GRIFFIN. *(as he starts to do so)* Get down!

(*to* **MR. GRIFFIN** *as the wheezing* **CONNELLY** *drops down again.*)

It's just as much MY fantasy as it is yours!

MR. GRIFFIN. Well, we've been running it *your* way – now I want to put in *my* two cents worth! *(to* **CONNELLY***)* Up!

MRS. GRIFFIN. Down!

(*The glassy-eyed* **CONNELLY** *pops up and down like a jack-in-the-box as the marital argument continues with* **MR. & MRS. GRIFFIN** *glaring at each other, eyeball to eyeball.*)

MR. GRIFFIN. I want you to stop –

MRS. GRIFFIN. I am *NOT* your servant!

MR. GRIFFIN. (*to* **CONNELLY**) UP!

MRS. GRIFFIN. (*flourishing her whip*) Down!

> (*As the weary* **CONNELLY** *plops down on his hands and knees again, we hear a smothered sneeze from closet 1.*)

BURGLAR'S VOICE. (*from closet*) Ah-choo!

CONNELLY. (*wheezing automatically*) Gezundheit.

MR. GRIFFIN. (*to* **MRS. GRIFFIN**) What was that?

MRS. GRIFFIN. (*impatiently*) The dog next door, probably; it's always –

MR. GRIFFIN. Didn't sound like a dog and it didn't sound next door. (*frowning suspiciously at closet 1*) Sounded like your closet.

MRS. GRIFFIN. (*still angry at him*) That is ridiculous! (*haughtily, marching to closet 1*) I can assure you (*starts to open closet door*) I am hiding nobody in my –

> (*She is startled into a backward leap at the sight of the* **BURGLAR**, *all tangled up with a mass of fur coats and looking rather like the abominable snowman.*)

Aaaaahhh!

BURGLAR. (*as jumpy as she is*) Don't *do* that, lady!

> (*They stare, dumbfounded, as he steps out of the closet still clutching the furs, and blurts out nervously.*)

All right folks, don't get excited, I've got a gun.

MRS. GRIFFIN. A *GUN!*

BURGLAR. (*starting*) You've got to stop doing that, lady, I'm an extremely nervous person. No loud noises no sudden movements…

> (*Behind the* **BURGLAR**, **CONNELLY** *crawls rapidly towards the drapes.*)

Stay close together now, so I can keep an eye on you…

> (**CONNELLY** *hides behind the drape.*)

Did I mention I have a gun?

(as **MRS. GRIFFIN** *nods unhappily)*

Just checking.

MR. GRIFFIN. *(disapprovingly)* You're a thief.

MRS. GRIFFIN. He's taken all my fur coats…

BURGLAR. They better be real, lady – because if you think it's any fun being cooped up in that closet…

MRS. GRIFFIN. How…how long were you in there?

BURGLAR. Long enough. *(a pause as he eyes them)* You're a real bunch of weirdos, you know that? And it's *me* they lock up.

MR. GRIFFIN. I hardly think a thief is the best judge of –

BURGLAR. I'm not a *thief* I'm a *burglar.* A thief works the streets, a burglar works the –

MR. GRIFFIN. You call this work?

BURGLAR. It's a lot harder than making business calls. which is mostly what you do, isn't it? When you're not being a closet queen, I mean.

MR. GRIFFIN. *(furiously)* Now listen, you –

MRS. GRIFFIN. Dear – he's got a gun.

MR. GRIFFIN. I don't believe it!

BURGLAR. *(fumbling with fur coats)* It's under here some-where…

MR. GRIFFIN. A man's character is in his eyes – this man is lying!

BURGLAR. It's all this damn fur…

MR. GRIFFIN. When I say go, we rush him – *(crouches)* Go!

(Nobody – including **MR. GRIFFIN** *– moves.)*

BURGLAR. *(finally extracting an automatic pistol from the fur)* See? See the gun?

MRS. GRIFFIN. *(to her husband)* You're a great judge of char-acter.

MR. GRIFFIN. *(staring numbly at pistol, which is pointed at him)* That's my gun.

MRS. GRIFFIN. I knew there'd be trouble if we had one lying around! Why did you have to get it?

MR. GRIFFIN. For burglars.

BURGLAR. And I appreciate it, I really do. *(suddenly realizes* **CONNELLY** *is missing)* Where's the heavy breather?

MRS. GRIFFIN. I'm sure I don't know to whom –

> *(We hear the ringing of a cellphone coming from behind the drape.* **BURGLAR** *points his gun at the drape as the ringing continues.)*

BURGLAR. Out from the drapes, Romeo!

> *(***CONNELLY** *emerges.)*

Over here, with the others…Now let's get this business –

> *(The phone keeps ringing.)*

That phone is getting on my nerves.

CONNELLY. It's the wife. She'll keep it up 'til I answer.

BURGLAR. *(waving gun)* Get rid of her quick, and be careful of what you say!

CONNELLY. *(into phone)* OK, I'm here…Well, I'm busy, it's a busy day. Yeah, I've got it right here… *(pulls grocery list from pocket, reads)* Bananas, onions, Handiwipes – peanut butter? OK, I'll add it to the list. *(fumbles for pencil)* You want the chunky or –

> *(hastily, as the exasperated* **BURGLAR** *menaces him with the gun)*

Listen, got to go now – plumbing emergency –

> *(The* **BURGLAR** *grabs the cellphone, pushes the disconnect button, sits shakily on the bed.)*

BURGLAR. I'm getting too old for this line of work. I kept hoping you kooks would go away. Why couldn't you just go –

> *(His gun twitches spasmodically as one of them moves slightly.)*

No sudden moves! I'm getting nervous again.

CONNELLY. *(anxiously eyeing the twitching pistol)* Don't be nervous.

BURGLAR. I can't help it.

MRS. GRIFFIN. *(soothingly)* There's nothing to be nervous about.

BURGLAR. It's my ulcer.

MRS. GRIFFIN. You have an ulcer?

MR. GRIFFIN. I have one, too – I'll give you something for it.

BURGLAR. *(eyeing him gloomily)* Anything you take, I don't want… *(muttering to himself as his gun continues to twitch)* Alright, don't panic nothing to worry about – I'm in control of the situation – *(standing up briskly)* And so we move on! The next step is…

(He falters.)

The next step…

(His eyes go blank.)

I can't think straight with all you people – I'm used to working alone…Drawers…desks… *(suddenly remembers)* Suitcase! That's it!

MRS. GRIFFIN. Suitcase?

BURGLAR. To put the stuff in – saw one in your hall closet. Get it! *(waves gun at her)* And put that whip down – it's making me nervous.

(She does so, starts to exit from bedroom.)

And remember, I've got your…

(uncertainly, as he eyes the square-jawed, stiffly erect **MR. GRIFFIN** *in his dress and high-heeled shoes)*

Well, whatever he is, I've got him – so no funny ideas.

MRS. GRIFFIN. *(heading for hall closet)* Just don't be nervous…

BURGLAR. *(to* **MR. GRIFFIN** *and* **CONNELLY***)* You can start emptying your pockets.

MR. GRIFFIN. *(with stern dignity)* I have no pockets.

BURGLAR. *(grimly)* Well, you'd better find some – *(pointing gun at him)* and there better be something in them… and I'm not talking about small change.

MR. GRIFFIN. If you didn't have that gun!

BURGLAR. But I *do* – thanks to you. *(to* **MRS. GRIFFIN** *returning with suitcase)* Put it on the bed and open it. *(as she does so)* Now you can get your jewels.

MRS. GRIFFIN. You've *already* got my furs!

BURGLAR. *(wearily)* Look, lady – I've done solitary for stealing a guard's watch – but it's nothing like being cooped up in a hot closet, tickled by fur, trying to hold back a sneeze, and being forced to listen to the ravings of a bunch of sex maniacs! My nerves are shot, my stomach is upset – and while you could never pay me enough to make up for the experience, I'm gonna make damn sure that you *do your best!*

MRS. GRIFFIN. But – I have no jewels…

BURGLAR. *(as his gun begins to twitch)* You're activating my ulcer…

MRS. GRIFFIN. *(moving to table with alacrity)* I'll get them.

BURGLAR. *(waving his gun at* **MR. GRIFFIN** *)* Money!

(As **MR. GRIFFIN** *glumly goes to closet to get his wallet,* **CONNELLY** *timidly raises his hand.)*

What's your problem?

CONNELLY. Well, I don't really belong here – I'm a working man like yourself, so to speak – so I was wondering if –

BURGLAR. No!

CONNELLY. No?

BURGLAR. I know all about you, lover boy – get it up! And I'm *talking* about your *wallet!*

(He stuffs furs in suitcase as they approach with wallets and jewel case.)

Put the valuables in the suitcase.

(watches **MR. GRIFFIN** *extract a wad of bills from his wallet)*

Now that's more like it!

(as **MRS. GRIFFIN** *reluctantly drops in a single piece of jewelry from her case)*

Just dump the whole box in – I'll sort it out later.

(*She does so with a look of pure hate and the others drop in their cash.*)

That's it, every little bit counts…(*confessing nervously as he clicks the suitcase shut*) You know, I never used a gun before – I specialize in empty apartments… (*goes to bedroom telephone wire*) But I'm not doing too bad, am I?

(*He appears anxious for approval. They don't seem eager to give it.*)

Alright, lover boy – make yourself useful. (*waves gun at* **CONNELLY**) The phone wire.

CONNELLY. Huh?

BURGLAR. Rip it out. (*as* **CONNELLY** *stares unhappily at the wire*) Now!

CONNELLY. But… (*moving reluctantly to wire*) what will the management say?

BURGLAR. You want to be around to find out?

CONNELLY. (*muttering as he tugs at the wire*) How did I get into this?

(*The wire comes away from the wall and he stares at the torn end.*)

I came up to fix the radiator.

BURGLAR. Now do the living room phone and the intercom wire – (*waves gun at him*) And remember – I'm jumpy.

CONNELLY. OK, OK.

BURGLAR. (*at bedroom door, muttering nervously to the* **GRIFFINS** *as he watches* **CONNELLY** *carry out his instructions*) I couldn't do this on a regular basis…too much to think about, so many details… (*as* **CONNELLY** *finishes*) Alright – back here with the others!

(*as* **CONNELLY** *re-joins the* **GRIFFINS**)

I think that's all…

(*anxiously to the* **GRIFFINS**)

BURGLAR. *(cont.)* Did I forget anything?

> *(They eye him stonily.)*

> Well, then – *(reaching for suitcase;)* I suppose that about wraps it up – *(stops, frowns at* **MRS. GRIFFIN**'s *hand)* Alright, lady – nice try.

MRS. GRIFFIN. *(hauteur)* I beg your pardon?

BURGLAR. The ring.

MRS. GRIFFIN. *(looking down at it)* But…that's my engagement ring!

BURGLAR. *(after a pause, indicating* **MR. GRIFFIN**) To him?

> *(She nods tremulously.)*

> I should think –

> *(***BURGLAR*** pries off ring.)*

> you wouldn't want to be reminded.

MRS. GRIFFIN. You'll never get away with this!

BURGLAR. *(putting ring in pocket)* Maybe – but if you're thinking of following me or screaming your heads off in the hall – *(reaches for suitcase)* I'm a three-time loser and very nervous, so all that will probably happen is that you get somebody shot… *(picks suitcase up)* Besides, I shouldn't think you want the neighbors to see you like this… *(starts backing out of bedroom)* Don't bother to see me out.

MRS. GRIFFIN. We'll report you to the police!

BURGLAR. *(backing into living room)* I'd be insulted if you didn't. Luckily, *(indicating his gloves)* I didn't leave any prints.

MRS. GRIFFIN. We'll *describe* you to them – your shifty brown eyes –

MR. GRIFFIN. Grey.

BURGLAR. *Hazel.*

CONNELLY. I thought they was green.

BURGLAR. That's the way, folks… *(backing through living room)* Keep up the good – *Aaaahhhh!*

(He trips over the tool-case, which had been left in the middle of the floor, teeters, claws frantically at the air, and falls over backwards, landing with a thump which knocks the air out of him and sends the gun skittering across the floor.)

(The **GRIFFINS** *come charging out of the bedroom, with* **CONNELLY** *cautiously in the rear.* **MRS. GRIFFIN** *retrieves the gun while* **MR. GRIFFIN** *pins the stunned* **BURGLAR***'s shoulders to the floor as* **CONNELLY** *approaches.)*

CONNELLY. *(sitting on the* **BURGLAR***)* I got him!

(The **BURGLAR** *groans, and* **MRS. GRIFFIN** *quickly comes over and points the gun down at him.)*

MRS. GRIFFIN. *(nervously but firmly)* Don't you move!

BURGLAR. *(feebly, from under* **CONNELLY***'s bulk)* Are you kidding? Get him off me, will you? I can't breathe…

MRS. GRIFFIN. It's all right, Mr. Connelly… *(gripping the gun with both hands)* I've got him covered.

BURGLAR. *(as* **CONNELLY** *climbs laboriously off him)* Take it easy with that thing, lady.

MR. GRIFFIN. *(holding his hand out for the gun)* Better let me have it.

(She gives it to him and he points it at the **BURGLAR***.)*

Get up slowly and be very *very* careful – *(holding the gun six inches from the* **BURGLAR***'s head)* I'm an expert shot.

BURGLAR. *(hastily)* I'm convinced *(starting to struggle up)* Just don't get nervous.

MRS. GRIFFIN. *(frowning as the* **BURGLAR** *reaches his hands and knees)* I think he ought to stay on the floor.

(The **BURGLAR** *hesitates.)*

On TV police dramas, they make them lie down, with their legs spread.

(The **BURGLAR***, with a resigned sigh, begins to lower himself again as* **MR. GRIFFIN** *says firmly.)*

MR. GRIFFIN. They don't always do that – *(to the* BURGLAR*)* I told you to *get up*!

(The BURGLAR *starts to push himself up.)*

More often, they lean them up against the wall, palms out, feet wide apart.

MRS. GRIFFIN. But he's so much safer on the *floor*.

MR. GRIFFIN. *(as the* BURGLAR *hesitates again)* He's just as safe against the *wall* – and he's much easier to search that way.

MRS. GRIFFIN. All you'd have to do is bend over and –

MR. GRIFFIN. *(stiffly)* It's not a question of bending over – it's a question of who wears the pants in this family!

(Glares at BURGLAR, *who has been staying patiently on his hands and knees.)*

Well? What are you waiting for?

BURGLAR. You got it worked out yet?

MR. GRIFFIN. *Up* against the *wall* – move it!

(The BURGLAR *resignedly leans against the indicated wall.)*

All right, Connelly – frisk him!

*(*CONNELLY *approaches him nervously, hesitates.)*

CONNELLY. What am I frisking for?

MRS. GRIFFIN. *(firmly)* You can start with my engagement ring.

CONNELLY. Right! *(rummages in pockets)* Item – *(brings ring out)* one ring. *(gives it to her, rummages about again)* Item – *(brings something else out)* one rabbit's foot.

BURGLAR. *(disgusted mutter)* Throw it away…

MR. GRIFFIN. Quiet!

CONNELLY. *(really throwing himself into the frisking business)* Item – one pack of Kleenex…*(examining it judiciously)* which has been slightly –

MR. GRIFFIN. Never mind that stuff – weapons, man, weapons!

CONNELLY. *Right. (starts moving his hands all over the* **BURGLAR***'s body)* Aha! *(brings out small pocket case of lock picks)* I believe we have Exhibit A here...

MR. GRIFFIN. What is it?

CONNELLY. *(putting case on coffee table)* Burglar tools, unless I miss my –

MR. GRIFFIN. Is that everything?

CONNELLY. There's nothing left to frisk.

MR. GRIFFIN. *(to* **BURGLAR***)* All right, you can turn around – slowly.

(The **BURGLAR** *does so and stands there with a hang-dog expression as they look at him.)*

MRS. GRIFFIN. What should we do with him?

MR. GRIFFIN. Turn him over to the police, naturally.

BURGLAR. *(panicky)* Oh, – listen, I – *(His eye falls on the suitcase, and he rushes to it desperately.)*

MR. GRIFFIN. *(pointing gun at him)* Careful!

BURGLAR. *(feverishly opening suitcase)* I'll make a deal with you! Let me go and – *(pointing dramatically at contents of suitcase)* everything in there is yours – what do you say?

MR. GRIFFIN. *(eyeing the contents with a frown)* It was ours in the first place.

BURGLAR. *(as* **MRS. GRIFFIN** *starts to remove her belongings from suitcase)* The point is – it still is – I mean, I've given it all back, so nothing really happened, no harm was done, so why don't we –

CONNELLY. *(firmly)* You are a *perpetrator*.

MR. GRIFFIN. That's right!

CONNELLY. *(with a growing sense of self-importance)* You was caught red-handed in an act of *perpetration*.

BURGLAR. *(feebly)* I didn't –

CONNELLY. *(taking out notebook, pencil)* You are guilty of willful destruction of property to the extent of... *(scribbling in notebook)* two telephone wires, one intercom wire –

MRS. GRIFFIN. *(heading for bedroom with furs, jewelry case)* You crushed my furs...

BURGLAR. Sorry –

MR. GRIFFIN. *(retrieving his wallet)* You're a menace to society!

BURGLAR. *(astonished)* Me? A menace? I'm small change for Christ sake. – I mean, look at all those banking and Wall street crooks. *(emotionally)* What are you picking on *me* for?

MR. GRIFFIN. Nobody's –

BURGLAR. Can't you give me a break – you got your goods back and I never did anything like this before – *(rushing on before* **MR. GRIFFIN** *can say anything)* It's all those medical bills for my mother's condition piling up, you see – I was desperate I didn't want to do this, but I didn't know where else –

MR. GRIFFIN. I thought you were in prison as a three-time loser.

BURGLAR. Well… *(slight pause)* Mother's been under the weather for a long time and –

MR. GRIFFIN. *Bull!* Next you'll be telling me it's all the fault of the system, right, Connelly?

CONNELLY. Love it or leave it.

MR. GRIFFIN. *(frowning sternly in his dress and high-heeled shoes at the* **BURGLAR***)* It's people like *you* who are undermining the moral fiber of this country!

BURGLAR. *(protesting)* I never –

MR. GRIFFIN. Well, you're not getting away with it – you're going back to *prison* where you *belong!*

BURGLAR. *(sagging hopelessly)* Oh, Christ…I've got to sit down…can I sit down….

*(***MR. GRIFFIN*** frowningly nods assent. The* **BURGLAR** *sits dejectedly on the downstage corner of the bed and buries his face in his hands as* **MRS. GRIFFIN** *returns from replacing things in the bedroom and* **CONNELLY** *stops scribbling and puts away his pencil with a portentous air.)*

CONNELLY. *(tapping notebook)* The evidence has been duly noted.

(puts notebook away, drifts over to suitcase)

So, if you don't mind…

(gets his money from the suitcase)

I'll just retrieve my belongings –

(stuffs the bills in his pockets and picks up his tool kit)

and be on my –

MR. GRIFFIN. Put it down!

CONNELLY. Huh?

MR. GRIFFIN. You're not going anywhere!

CONNELLY. *(unhappily putting down tool kit)* But –

*(as **MRS. GRIFFIN** briskly tidies up, removing the rest of the cash from the suitcase)*

I've got to report this to the –

MR. GRIFFIN. *I'll* decide who reports *what when* and *where*!

MRS. GRIFFIN. Besides –

(snapping suitcase shut)

We're not finished with you yet, Mr. Connelly.

(picks suitcase up)

Have you forgotten?

(eyes him with a gently chiding expression)

You have a contract to fulfill…

CONNELLY. *(watching her take suitcase to hall closet)* Contract?

MRS. GRIFFIN. *(putting away suitcase)* Once things are back to normal.

CONNELLY. *(numbly, as she returns from hall)* You mean you – you –

MR. GRIFFIN. *(eyeing him gloomily)* So far he's been a total washout.

MRS. GRIFFIN. That's hardly fair.

CONNELLY. You still expect me to –

MRS. GRIFFIN. He hasn't really had a chance to get his *teeth* into –

BURGLAR. *(his head still buried in his hands)* License plates…

(They look at him.)

All those goddam license plates…

MR. GRIFFIN. What are you mumbling about?

BURGLAR. *(slowly raising his head, revealing hollow, despairing eyes)* You know what it means? It means I'll be making license plates for the rest of my life…

MRS. GRIFFIN. *(coming to him with a certain amount of compassion)* Ohh…

BURGLAR. *(with increasing hopelessness)* You know what that does to a man? Year after year of making license plates on the inside for cars on the outside…When I close my eyes at night, all I see are their numbers…That's when I *can* close my eyes…*(pulls his shirt collar down and points at neck)* See that?

MR. GRIFFIN. *(frowning)* What is it?

MRS. GRIFFIN. *(examining **BURGLAR***'s neck)* It seems to be some kind of scar – *(intrigued)* in the form of two capital letters –

BURGLAR. *(glumly)* In my last jail term, I had this cellmate… He wanted to be my playmate…

MRS. GRIFFIN. Playmate?

BURGLAR. He was hot for my body…Don't ask me why. Anyway, he was smaller than me, so I was able to fight him off – only, one night when I was asleep he managed to tie me up and – *(indicating the scar)* carve this for revenge.

MRS. GRIFFIN. *(reading from the scar)* F.U.?

BURGLAR. He had a filthy mouth…

MR. GRIFFIN. *(impatiently)* I think I've heard just about –

MRS. GRIFFIN. No, wait a minute dear – this is interesting – *(to the **BURGLAR**)* Didn't you ever succumb?

BURGLAR. *(uneasily)* Succumb?

MRS. GRIFFIN. To the sexual pressures that prisoners –

BURGLAR. They never got to *me* – I don't go for that stuff!

MRS. GRIFFIN. Really…*(eyes* **BURGLAR** *with an intrigued expression)* How much time have you spent in prison?

BURGLAR. *(mournfully)* Seventeen years total.

MRS. GRIFFIN. As a heterosexual?

BURGLAR. *(suspiciously)* A what?

MRS. GRIFFIN. You've continued to…desire women?

BURGLAR. Well, yeah – I was even married once, but she got tired of waitin' for –

MRS. GRIFFIN. How long was your last jail term?

BURGLAR. Five years.

MRS. GRIFFIN. When did you get out?

BURGLAR. *(unhappily)* This morning.

MRS. GRIFFIN. *(going excitedly to* **MR. GRIFFIN***)* Did you hear that! Do you realize what we have here – under our control?

MR. GRIFFIN. *(eyeing the* **BURGLAR** *with dawning awareness)* You mean…

MRS. GRIFFIN. – A libido that has been pent up for *five long years!*

BURGLAR. *(uneasily, as they stare at him)* A what?

MRS. GRIFFIN. You said yourself that Connelly has been a wash-out.

MR. GRIFFIN. So *far,* but I'm hoping that –

MRS. GRIFFIN. *(as* **CONNELLY** *shifts uncomfortably on his feet)* We both know Mr. Connelly has gone just about as far as he is capable of going…

(**CONNELLY** *looks increasingly uncomfortable.)*

As long as he was all we had to work with, we were forced to make do; but – *(beams happily at the* **BURGLAR***)* This could be just what we've been looking for, Charles – strong criminal tendencies…a seething cauldron of suppressed desire…

MRS. GRIFFIN. *(frowning at the* **BURGLAR***)* I don't know…

MRS. GRIFFIN. He's much closer to the ideal – he even has a scar –

MR. GRIFFIN. Suppose this one doesn't pan out either?

MRS. GRIFFIN. Nothing ventured, nothing gained.

BURGLAR. *(anxiously, as they approach him from different sides)* Say – what's goin' –

MRS. GRIFFIN. How would you like to avoid being sent back to prison?

BURGLAR. You mean – *(hope floods into his eyes)* you'll let me go?

MRS. GRIFFIN. Not yet – you'd simply go right back to burgling again. What we are proposing is more in the nature of... *amnesty.*

BURGLAR. *(uncomprehendingly)* Amnesty?

MRS. GRIFFIN. Which you will earn by performing certain... *(sits on the arm of the* **BURGLAR***'s easy chair)* services.

MR. GRIFFIN. *(pointing gun at* **BURGLAR***)* And you'd *better perform!*

BURGLAR. *(uneasily)* Perform?

MRS. GRIFFIN. Have you ever heard of...

(leaning towards the increasingly trapped-looking **BURGLAR** *with the air of sharing a wonderful revelation)*

Dr. Leopold Baumgartner?

(curtain)

End of Act One

ACT TWO

*(Shortly after. At rise: the positions are about the same. The **BURGLAR** is looking nervously up at the **GRIFFINS**.)*

BURGLAR. You mean – you really expect me to do what *(jerking a thumb at **CONNELLY**) he* was doing?

MRS. GRIFFIN. *(nodding serenely)* A lifetime of frustration has undoubtedly twisted you into a criminal, so this will be therapy for *you*, as well as –

BURGLAR. *(panicky)* No, no – I can't do that –

MRS. GRIFFIN. It's a chance to release all that pent-up heterosexuality –

BURGLAR. *(jumping up feverishly)* I'm not pent up! Believe me, I'm not pent up! And – and – whips make me nervous – my ulcer can't take whips –

MRS. GRIFFIN. Of course – *(getting up from arm chair)* if you'd rather spend the rest of your life making license plates –

BURGLAR. *(trapped expression)* Oh, Christ –

MRS. GRIFFIN. – and getting initials carved on you by rejected prison playmates – *(to **MR. GRIFFIN**, regretfully)* I'm afraid we'll have to turn him over to the police after –

BURGLAR. Wait! Wait a minute…

(He stares at them out of desperate hollow eyes and then, in a broken voice)

What…what would I have to do?

MRS. GRIFFIN. *(brightly)* Well, now! *(coming to him)* It's really quite simple… I am, of course, the beautiful vulnerable, highly desirable wife of a French –

MR. GRIFFIN. He heard all that from the closet – can't you speed it up?

MRS. GRIFFIN. I'm just firming up the outlines for him. *(takes the haggard-eyed* **BURGLAR** *by the arm)* Now all you have to do is –

(She gently draws the **BURGLAR** *– who wears the expression of a man on his way to the gallows – towards the bedroom as* **MR. GRIFFIN** *keeps the gun pointed at him.)*

– put your normal criminal tendencies and primitive animal drives into the role of Jacques –

CONNELLY. *(who is being completely ignored)* Hey –

MRS. GRIFFIN. – a brutish, low-browed, hairy –

CONNELLY. *Hey!*

(They turn to him.)

What about *me?*

MRS. GRIFFIN. *(vaguely, as though she'd forgotten about him)* Oh, Mr. Connelly…You can go.

CONNELLY. Go?

MRS. GRIFFIN. That's what you wanted, wasn't it – the painters in 5F and all that?

CONNELLY. *(uneasily)* Well…

MRS. GRIFFIN. You'd better see to them. *(starting to turn back to* **BURGLAR***)* I know we can rely on your discretion –

MR. GRIFFIN. *(to* **CONNELLY***)* Not a word to anyone!

CONNELLY. *(numbly)* Gotcha.…

(He slowly picks up his tool-case again, starts to turn.)

MRS. GRIFFIN. *(to* **BURGLAR***)* To get back to cases – *(guiding him toward bedroom)* behind your red-rimmed eyes, you are a seething volcano of pent-up heterosexuality…

*(***CONNELLY** *stops, looking rather pent-up himself.)*

…who has long felt a secret lust for my soft, white –

CONNELLY. *(blurting it out) I've* got a scar, *too!*

(They look at him blankly as he explains a bit anti-climactically)

Appendicitis…It's got no letters, but it's five inches long, which is unusual, and jagged around the edges

– what I mean is – *(with sudden emotion)* *I'm no washout!* *(pointing at* **BURGLAR***)* Anything *he* can handle, *I* can handle!

MRS. GRIFFIN. *(intrigued)* Why, Mr. Connelly –

CONNELLY. *(thumping himself on the chest)* Sixteen years I been superintendent here – I pay my taxes – I take care of all kinds of tenant problems and emergencies – *(glares indignantly at* **BURGLAR***)* – anything a common *criminal* can handle – *I* can handle!

MRS. GRIFFIN. You're *jealous!* – *(to* **MR. GRIFFIN***, with glowing eyes)* Did you hear that, dear? He's *jealous!*

MR. GRIFFIN. *(exasperatedly)* Aren't we ever going to get this show on the –

MRS. GRIFFIN. But now we have some *back-up* insurance – *(comes glowingly up to* **CONNELLY***)* now that we see what Mr. Connelly is really made of!

CONNELLY. I just want credit where credit is –

MRS. GRIFFIN. *(taking the tool case from him)* And you shall *have* it, Mr. Connelly – We're taking you back on the team!

CONNELLY. *(uneasily)* Team?

MR. GRIFFIN. *(gesturing with gun at* **BURGLAR***)* What about this one?

MRS. GRIFFIN. He's still our most promising candidate… *(thoughtfully eyes the hollow-eyed* **BURGLAR***)* I'm banking a lot on those pent-up desires – but still – *(to* **MR. GRIFFIN***)* you're always talking about the need for alternate options…

MR. GRIFFIN. *(frowning)* You mean –

MRS. GRIFFIN. If he should turn out to be a…flat tire, so to speak – *(indicating* **CONNELLY***)* Mr. Connelly can 'be our spare!

CONNELLY. *(increasing uneasiness)* Spare?

MR. GRIFFIN. *(eyeing him sourly)* Assuming he can pump himself up.

CONNELLY. Uh…just a minute –

BURGLAR. *(hastily)* He can have my place – I'll be the spare.

MR. GRIFFIN. Quiet!

CONNELLY. Uh – Mr. Griffin – Mrs. Griffin – I think we got a communications problem here… *(floundering nervously as they look at him)* When I said I could do anything *he* could do, I didn't mean he couldn't *do* it, I just meant I could do it, too – *if* I had the time – That's the thing, you see… *(drifts towards his tool box as they look increasingly impatient)* It's not just the painters, it's the window sash, so – *(picks up tool box)* while I'd like to oblige with some spare tire duty, I'm afraid –

MR. GRIFFIN. Put it down.

CONNELLY. I'm sure he'll come through with –

MR. GRIFFIN. *(pointing gun at him)* Down!

(**CONNELLY** *obeys with alacrity.*)

This whole thing is getting disorganized – too many chiefs and not enough Indians… Now! *(points gun at* **BURGLAR***)* You are going to perform – or else! *(to* **CONNELLY***) You* are going to stay on tap – just in case. Is that clear? *(to* **MRS. GRIFFIN**, *as they nod unhappily) Now* can we get moving?

MRS. GRIFFIN. Certainly. *(drawing the trapped-looking* **BURGLAR** *into the bedroom)* I'll set him up.

CONNELLY. *(following her, to* **BURGLAR***)* You're gonna to be just fine – there's nothing to be nervous about.

MRS. GRIFFIN. *(leading* **BURGLAR** *to drapes)* Just follow your normal criminal instincts.

CONNELLY. *(the old "pro" instructing the novice)* What you do is, you get behind your drapes…

(The **BURGLAR** *stares nervously at* **CONNELLY** *and* **MR. GRIFFIN**, *who is crossing the bedroom towards him in his high heels with a stern expression.)*

And I generally start with a little heavy breathing – you know, like background –

BURGLAR. *(nervously, to* **MRS. GRIFFIN***)* You expect me to perform with… *them* here?

MRS. GRIFFIN. *(soothingly)* My husband will be in the closet…

CONNELLY. *(starting for closet 1)* I'll be making observations from the other one.

MRS. GRIFFIN. Be careful of my furs!

CONNELLY. *(entering closet 1)* Right. *(closes door)*

MR. GRIFFIN. *(at closet 2)* I'll be watching every move you make. *(enters closet)* And remember – *(turns to face the* **BURGLAR** *with the gun)* I'm an expert shot!

MRS. GRIFFIN. *(picking up her whip)* The important thing is to be spontaneous.

BURGLAR. Spontaneous…

(He watches with increasing nervousness as she tucks the bull whip under the bed pillow.)

Jesus…Listen, suppose I – I do my best, but I just can't perform the way you want me to –

MR. GRIFFIN. *(from closet 2)* License plates.

MRS. GRIFFIN. *(with gentle compassion, as the* **BURGLAR** *stares at the closet door)* I'm afraid he's right.

BURGLAR. *(turning his haggard gaze to her)* You mean – you'd really turn me in?

MRS. GRIFFIN. You'd leave us no choice. *(Smiles reassuringly as the* **BURGLAR** *looks increasingly tense.)* But I'm sure you won't let us down… *(starts to push him behind drapes)* So if you'll just take up your position –

BURGLAR. *(desperately)* You got a Playboy?

MRS. GRIFFIN. *(taken aback)* I beg your pardon?

BURGLAR. Or Penthouse or any of that kind of… *(with groping defensiveness as she looks at him)* That's all we had in the slammer, you see, centerfolds…It would help get me in the mood… *(as she continues to stare blankly at him)* I don't need a whole centerfold, actually; any of those pictures would do the –

MRS. GRIFFIN. *(frostily)* A picture is two-dimensional. *I* am three-dimensional.

BURGLAR. I know, but – it's all in what you're used to, right? *(shrugs helplessly)* I spent a lot of years with those centerfolds…

MR. GRIFFIN. *(from closet 2, gloomily)* It doesn't sound promising.

MRS. GRIFFIN. But if he just needs it to get himself…*(gropes for word; then, to closet 1)* Mr. Connelly?

CONNELLY. *(from closet)* Revved up.

MRS. GRIFFIN. Is that it?

BURGLAR. Uh-huh.

MRS. GRIFFIN. *(to closet 2)* Why not let him try, dear? We've gone this far.

MR. GRIFFIN. Get on with it!

MRS. GRIFFIN. *(going to magazine rack)* I'm afraid all we have to give you is… *(rummaging through magazines)* a *Vogue.*

BURGLAR. *Vogue?*

MRS. GRIFFIN. *(bringing it to him)* You'll have to make do with a lingerie ad.

BURGLAR. Oh. Well… *(morosely leafing through magazine)* I'll do my best.

MRS. GRIFFIN. *(going to her vanity table) Places,* everybody!

(The **BURGLAR** *steps behind the drapes with his* Vogue. *She sits at the vanity, starts slowly, sensuously, brushing her hair.)*

MRS. GRIFFIN. *(cont.)* Here I am again…alone in my boudoir…waiting fearfully for the return of my husband, the Marquis…There is nobody in the chateau but Jacques, the swineherd… *(brush, brush)* in whose eyes, I have sometimes detected what seems almost like the flame of desire as he bows before me… *(brush, brush, brush)* I'm sure it must be my imagination, fed by those stories of rampaging – *(stops brushing, then, tremulously)* But what is that sound – the sound of heavy, breathing… *(pause, then, rather crisply)* I was sure I heard *heavy, labored breathing…*

(a wheezing sound from behind the drapes and her voice becomes tremulous again)

Can that be my imagination, too? *(She turns fearfully,*

stares at the drapes.) It appears to be coming from behind those drapes…*(slowly stands up)* There seems to be someone there – and he's coming out – *(increased wheezing and agitation of drapes)* Oh, Mon Dieu – *(terrified whisper)* He's *coming out…*

*(The **BURGLAR** emerges from behind the drapes, wheezing nervously, his eyes glued to a lingerie ad.)*

MRS. GRIFFIN. Jacques! *(terror-stricken)* Why are you looking at me like that…What do you want… *(backs towards her bed)* Why are you advancing towards me…

(He stands there, wheezing away, eyes still glued to the Vogue *like a security blanket.)*

…*advancing* towards me!

*(The **BURGLAR** starts nervously and wanders off in the wrong direction, still wheezing, eyes still glued to the* Vogue.*)*

MR. GRIFFIN. *(from closet 2)* Not that way!

CONNELLY. *(from closet 1, as the **BURGLAR** wanders off at another tangent)* More to the right.

MRS. GRIFFIN. *(frowning, as the **BURGLAR** bumps into a chair)* What *is* the matter with you?

BURGLAR. *(desperately)* It's not me – it's the pictures!

MRS. GRIFFIN. Pictures?

BURGLAR. They're not like Playboy Playmates – They're too skinny – *(rushes with magazine to closet 2)* Look at 'em – *(holds the* Vogue *up to keyhole)* They look like a bunch of guys in drag –

*(hastily, as **MR. GRIFFIN** emerges from the closet with the gun)*

No offence, it's just – well, I wouldn't need pictures if this was my kind of situation, but – I just can't get with that French stuff. I mean…being a swineherd just don't turn me on.

MRS. GRIFFIN. *(hurt)* Don't you have…*any* interest in ravishing me?

BURGLAR. Nothing personal, it's just – well, you're calling all the shots… *(nervously, to* **MR. GRIFFIN***)* It's hard for a man to function when a woman's calling the shots.

MRS. GRIFFIN. That depends on the man.

MR. GRIFFIN. *(to* **MRS. GRIFFIN***, sternly)* You see what you've done? You've made him part of the *problem* instead of part of the *solution.* *(muttering to himself)* That's what comes of delegating responsibility, if you want something done *right,* do it your –

MRS. GRIFFIN. I'm doing my best…I'm trying as hard as I know how to… *(turns away from him on the verge of tears)* save a marriage…

(After a second, **MR. GRIFFIN***. goes to her, as though not unaffected by his wife's emotion.)*

MR. GRIFFIN. I know you are, Livvy. And now that I'm standing in your shoes, so to speak, I can see how difficult it must be to be a woman. You mustn't blame yourself for what we've been going through. I assure you that you are still a beautiful, desirable woman. However, the way things are going right now… *(with quiet but deeply-felt concern)* I'm afraid we're never going to get to the ravishing part.

MRS. GRIFFIN. *(fleeting look of pain)* Don't say that.

(As the troubled married couple stare at each other, **CONNELLY** *cautiously opens the door of closet 1 while the* **BURGLAR** *edges longingly toward the bathroom window fire escape.)*

MRS. GRIFFIN. I believe in *us.*

MR. GRIFFIN. *(after a pause in which they look searchingly at each other)* So do I. *(with a tender smile)* Your nose is shiny. Why don't you go freshen up, and I'll get things moving here.

MRS. GRIFFIN. *(dabbing at her tear-stained face)* All right.

(She thoughtfully eyes the **BURGLAR***, who freezes in his tracks as* **MR. GRIFFIN** *turns toward him with the gun again.)*

Do you think you can make him functional?

MR. GRIFFIN. I didn't get where I am today without learning how to handle men.

CONNELLY. *(sticking his head out of closet 1 as* **MRS. GRIFFIN** *disappears into the bathroom)* Can I please go home?

MR. GRIFFIN. *No.* You're still on tap.

(He waves his gun at the **BURGLAR** *as* **CONNELLY***'s head retreats inside the closet.)*

Come over here!

(The **BURGLAR** *does so with trepidation.)*

What's your name?

BURGLAR. Lapchick.

MR. GRIFFIN. Well, Lapchick…

(He puts his arm around the **BURGLAR***'s shoulder and starts walking him around the bedroom in the fatherly attitude of a senior executive with a junior employee of the firm.)*

How long have you been with us now?

BURGLAR. About an hour.

MR. GRIFFIN. You know, Lapchick, I don't believe in chance, do you?

BURGLAR. *(uncertainly)* Well –

MR. GRIFFIN. *(continuing to stroll him around)* Losers believe in chance. Winners *make* their chances and *take* their chances. *(stops, looks at* **BURGLAR***)* You've been a loser, Lapchick, now you have a chance to be a *winner.*

BURGLAR. *(suspiciously)* I have?

MR. GRIFFIN. A chance to do something decent for the first time in your life…by helping this fine woman over her delicate emotional problem.

BURGLAR. Her problem? I thought it was yours.

MR. GRIFFIN. *(stopping with a frown)* You're not concentrating, Chapwick. You're never going to be a winner in the game of life unless you learn to *concentrate.*

BURGLAR. Sorry.

MR. GRIFFIN. As I was saying…women have all these complicated glands and chemical shiftings about which are continually messing up their emotions – *(confidentially)* we can thank God, Chapwick, that we have sensible insides.

BURGLAR. I guess so, only when my ulcer –

MR. GRIFFIN. Which explains our superior stability and problem-solving powers. *Now* – when my wife, because of unsound interior engineering, suddenly developed this problem of feeling completely undesirable, I sensed it immediately, of course. So powerful was her feeling of undesirability that nothing I could say or do would change it…It ended up affecting me so that…I was no longer *capable* of desiring her…and such was my loyalty to her…that I could no longer desire any woman…

BURGLAR. Because of all that chemical stuff?

MR. GRIFFIN. Exactly. Now tell me, Chapchick – did I have any right to let my wife's delicate emotional problem ruin our chance for happiness? Would *you* if you were in my shoes?

BURGLAR. Uh – *(eyeing the shoes)* I don't suppose so…

MR. GRIFFIN. Spoken like a winner! I knew you'd understand why I kept searching until I found Dr. Baumgartner and why, if you help me make this fine woman a healthy, whole person again, I'll make you the Aleutian Islands field representative of Better Ball Bearings with full perks including a Class A expense account.

BURGLAR. Class A?

MR. GRIFFIN. *(expansively)* And if you won't help, it's a future full of license plates… *(holds out his hand)* Deal?

BURGLAR. *(grabbing his hand)* I'll take it.

MR. GRIFFIN. *(suddenly the impatient field general again)* Then *Let's get cracking!*

BURGLAR. *(uneasily, as **MRS. GRIFFIN** emerges from the bathroom)* Cracking?

MR. GRIFFIN. Concentrate on finding something that revs you up and turns you on. Besides Playboy, I mean.

MRS. GRIFFIN. *(coming to the* **BURGLAR***)* Some memory or imagined situation that sets your pulse to pounding... causing that little vein in your forehead to swell and throb with the heat of your crazed animal lust – *(stops herself with an effort)* Haven't you got anything like that?

BURGLAR. Well....

MR. GRIFFIN. *(with executive efficiency)* I'll give you one: a dormitory in a school for wayward girls with –

*(***BURGLAR*** shakes his head.)*

A Roman orgy?

*(***BURGLAR*** looks even more morose.)*

An Arab oil sheik's orgy?

(He frowns at the **BURGLAR***'s continued lack of enthusiasm.)*

Well – what does turn you on?

BURGLAR. *(after a pause)* Prison.

MRS. GRIFFIN. Prison?

MR. GRIFFIN. *(disgustedly)* I thought you were a heterosexual.

BURGLAR. I am. But the Warden's got this beautiful –

MRS. GRIFFIN. *(excitedly)* Wife! Of course – a lovely, vulnerable woman surrounded by a thousand sex-starved –

BURGLAR. An old hag.

MRS. GRIFFIN. The warden's daughter then, unaware in her innocence of –

BURGLAR. *(shaking his head)* A young hag.

MR. GRIFFIN. Then who –

BURGLAR. The maid.

MRS. GRIFFIN. *(slight frown)* Maid?

BURGLAR. She's Puerto Rican..

MRS. GRIFFIN. *(stiffly)* A Puerto Rican maid. *(with an effort)* That's all right – I can adjust to that...Tell me about her.

BURGLAR. Well...I saw her when I was sent to wax the Warden's floors – *(to* **MR. GRIFFIN***)* That's before they discovered I was allergic to floor wax... *(looks out, remembering)* That maid was really well built...I used to watch her dust...

MRS. GRIFFIN. Dust?

BURGLAR. Sometimes, she had to dust something like a coffee table and she'd bend over real low and –

MRS. GRIFFIN. *(nodding happily)* the top of her low-cut blouse would fall away, revealing her –

BURGLAR. *(shaking his head)* She had her back to me.

MRS. GRIFFIN. Back?

BURGLAR. That's the view I prefer, actually, when they're built like *she* is – you know – *(pantomimes a woman's large behind with his hands)* with something a man can really –

MRS. GRIFFIN. *(sudden insight)* You're a "buttocks" man rather than a "breasts" man! *(to* **MR. GRIFFIN***)* Remember Dr. Baumgartner's chapter on that?

MR. GRIFFIN. *(to the uncomfortable-looking* **BURGLAR***)* No reason to be embarrassed – it's a perfectly acceptable erogenous zone.

BURGLAR. *(nervously)* Right.

MRS. GRIFFIN. How does it go?

BURGLAR. Go?

MR. GRIFFIN. The *fantasy.*

BURGLAR. Right. Well...I'll be laying in bed sometimes and I'll...I'll have this dream...

MRS. GRIFFIN. *(encouragingly)* Yes?

BURGLAR. I'm doing the warden's floors – with the waxing machine, you know – and I gradually work my way into the bedroom...

MRS. GRIFFIN. Of course...

BURGLAR. And I'll see the maid there – her name is Rosita –

MRS. GRIFFIN. *(trying to get the "feel" of the fantasy)* Rosita...

BURGLAR. She's dusting...

MRS. GRIFFIN. *(managing to make it sound erotic)* Dusting ..

BURGLAR. ...with one of those feather dusters. I...work the machine closer to her...

MRS. GRIFFIN. Closer....

BURGLAR. And closer...

MRS. GRIFFIN. And then?

BURGLAR. Well, then she...she bends over to dust something real low, , you know and...well. *(pantomimes a large behind only a few inches away)* there it is –

MRS. GRIFFIN. *(hushed whisper, getting caught up in the fantasy)* Tempting you...

BURGLAR. *(staring dazedly at the invisible behind)* Uh-huh...

MRS. GRIFFIN. Calling to you...

BURGLAR. Uh-huh...

MR. GRIFFIN. *(a bit impatiently)* And then?

BURGLAR. Then I...I reach out...

MRS. GRIFFIN. Slowly...

BURGLAR. Uh-huh...slowly...and –

MRS. GRIFFIN. And?

BURGLAR. *(with a sense of dazed erotic arousal)* I pinch it...

MRS. GRIFFIN. And then?

BURGLAR. Then?

MRS. GRIFFIN. *(at a peak of anticipation)* What happens then?

BURGLAR. *(turning to her, matter-of-factly)* That's when I wake up.

MRS. GRIFFIN. *(slight pause)* Wake up? You mean –

MR. GRIFFIN. That's the most boring fantasy I've ever heard!

MRS. GRIFFIN. Well... *(half-heartedly)* I did think the beginning had a certain primitive –

MR. GRIFFIN. *Boring!*

MRS. GRIFFIN. We haven't really given it a chance to –

MR. GRIFFIN. What chance? One pinch and he's finished!

MRS. GRIFFIN. That's not true! *(eyeing the BURGLAR with compassion)* You've been practicing psycho-sexual censorship, haven't you?

BURGLAR. *(uneasily)* Huh?

MRS. GRIFFIN. No need to deny it, We understand…

MR. GRIFFIN. *(frowning)* Understand what?

MRS. GRIFFIN. It's in his face, Charles – can't you see?

(**MR. GRIFFIN** *suspiciously examines the face of the* **BURGLAR.**)

MRS. GRIFFIN. *(cont.)* The tense, haunted expression of a man who has been forced to inhibit even his fantasies – and why? *(with feeling)* because he has been locked up for years in a cage…because to even *dream* of what he wanted to do would release such a pent-up dam of frustrations that they would literally *tear him apart…* *(eyes the* **BURGLAR** *glowingly)* But now he is out of the cage…Now when I become Rosita, the Puerto Rican maid of his dreams… *(steps close to the* **BURGLAR**) his unconscious will know it is free to let a pinch be…not the *end (takes his arm)* but the *beginning…*

MR. GRIFFIN. *(grudgingly, moving to his closet)* We'll see.

BURGLAR. *(to* **MRS. GRIFFIN**, *nervously)* You're gonna be Rosita?

MRS. GRIFFIN. Si. *(drawing him towards the drapes)* The dark-eyed señorita who makes the wax melt in your machine.

BURGLAR. Machine?

MRS. GRIFFIN. *(positioning the* **BURGLAR** *in front of the drapes)* You're just outside the bedroom door, waxing floors, and then you see me inside dusting, and you let nature take its course – ready?

BURGLAR. *(tense mutter)* I suppose so…

MRS. GRIFFIN. *(going to her vanity)* Let the dam burst…Open those floodgates…

MR. GRIFFIN. *(to* **BURGLAR**, *from inside his closet)* Function – or *else!*

(*He closes the closet door on himself.*)

MRS. GRIFFIN. Curtain.

(She immediately strikes the attitude of a slightly bent-over maid, sticking her behind out, holding an imaginary feather duster and exclaiming in a thick, Latino voice.)

Here I om, all alone in thee house of thee Warden in thee meedle of thee preeson...

(The **BURGLAR** *emits a strange humming sound as he holds his arms out.)*

surrounded by all these creemeenals – *(She breaks off and frowns at the humming* **BURGLAR.***)* What are you doing?

BURGLAR. The sound of the waxing machine.

MRS. GRIFFIN. *(unhappily)* Do we have to have it?

BURGLAR. *(shrugging helplessly)* It's not a waxing machine if it don't make noise.

MRS. GRIFFIN. Then let Mr. Connelly do it – I want you to concentrate on your lusts...*Mr. Connelly?* A little waxing machine, please?

(We hear a hum from closet 1.)

BURGLAR. Too high.

MRS. GRIFFIN. A little lower, Mr. Connelly.

(The hum lowers.)

Is that better?

BURGLAR. *(considering)* Well –

MRS. GRIFFIN. *(firmly)* It will have to do...From the top now. *(resumes her former attitude)* Curtain.

(She sticks her butt out, **CONNELLY** *resumes humming and the* **BURGLAR** *vibrates his arms as though they are holding a waxing machine.)*

Caramba! I om so nervous to be in thee house alone weeth thot veecious murderer Lopchick...

(The **BURGLAR** *does not appear happy with this description.)*

Sometimes there ees an expression een hees tiny, peeglike eyes – *(agitatedly flicks her imaginary duster at the vanity table)* I must not theenk about thot…He ees here to wox thee floors, thot ees all… *(moves about, flicking the duster)* I try not to theenk about all thee women he has attacked… *(flick, flick)* I try not to be norvous just because he ees coming into thee bedroom weeth hees woxing machine…

(She is close to the **BURGLAR**, *who nervously manipulates his waxing machine as* **CONNELLY** *keeps up an unsteady hum.)*

MRS. GRIFFIN. I weel keep my bock turned to heem so he cannot see how norvous I am…

(Sticks out her behind at the **BURGLAR**, *who stares at it uneasily from his original position in front of the drapes.)*

as he comes closer and closer and –

MR. GRIFFIN. *(from closet)* Move it!

(The **BURGLAR** *takes a jumpy step towards* **MRS. GRIFFIN**'s *behind.)*

MRS. GRIFFIN. *(horrified whisper)* Madre mia! I theenk he ees reaching out towards me ond I om paralyzed weeth fright as I stand here, unable to move, and I feel heem reaching out towards me weeth hees fingers…

(The **BURGLAR** *slowly extends a trembling hand towards* **GRIFFIN**'s *rear end.)*

I can almost feel them. Soon they weel be touching my soft, white, vulnerable –

MR. GRIFFIN. Well, go ahead – *pinch* her!

CONNELLY. *(from closet 1)* You can do it…

MRS. GRIFFIN. I om so frightened…

MR. GRIFFIN. *(as the* **BURGLAR**'s *hand shakes uncontrollably)* What are you waiting for?

CONNELLY. Just a few inches more…

MRS. GRIFFIN. *(backing her behind into the* **BURGLAR**'s *hand)* Santa Maria! He ees starting to *peench* me!

CONNELLY. Attaboy!

MR. GRIFFIN. *(disgustedly)* He's not doing anything.

CONNELLY. Squeeze your fingers together, that's all you –

BURGLAR. *(breaking away)* It's no use – I can't – I just can't…

MR. GRIFFIN. Now what's the matter?

BURGLAR. *(moving about distractedly)* I tried to do what you want me to do, but I'm a very nervous person and I've got an ulcer and I did my best but *(slumps onto chaise lounge)* I'm too old for this kind of activity…

MR. GRIFFIN. *(opening closet door)* You're younger than I am!

BURGLAR. *(head sunk dejectedly)* Well, if you'd done as much time as I have – It's like she says – sex in prison is more of a headache than anything else…unless you're queer…so…after a few years, you… *(shrugs morosely)* sort of lose the urge…

MR. GRIFFIN. *(coming out of closet)* Get ready, Connelly!

CONNELLY. *(from closet 1)* Oh, Jesus…

MRS. GRIFFIN. *(unbelievingly)* You mean to tell me you have no pent-up desires in prison – no secret, lustful yearnings?

BURGLAR. *(raising his head)* I didn't say that – Sure I do…

MRS. GRIFFIN. For what?

BURGLAR. *(after a slight pause)* Pepperoni pizza.

MRS. GRIFFIN. *(blankly)* Pizza?

BURGLAR. Ordered special, you know, with extra cheese and onions and lots of –

MR. GRIFFIN. *That* does it! *(to closet 1)* Connelly, get *out* here – on the double! *(as **CONNELLY** emerges unhappily from the closet)* You'd better be revved up because my patience is at an end!

CONNELLY. *(pointing angrily at **BURGLAR**)* It's all your fault!

BURGLAR. I didn't do anything.

CONNELLY. You can say that again!

BURGLAR. *(jumping up, stung)* Well, I didn't see you winning any medals – you're only good on a fire escape!

MR. GRIFFIN. *(as they glare at each other)* Never mind bickering about –

CONNELLY. At least I know how to pinch –

BURGLAR. Cigars – that's all you know how to pinch!

CONNELLY. Listen to who's talking about stealing!

MR. GRIFFIN. *(frowning at them)* Stop this –

BURGLAR. At least I'm an *honest* thief!

CONNELLY. *(nose to nose with him)* Oh, yeah?

BURGLAR. Yeah!

CONNELLY. Oh yeah –

MR. GRIFFIN. *That's enough!*

MRS. GRIFFIN. *(excitedly)* No, wait – I think we've got a real breakthrough – look at them, Charles!

(**CONNELLY** *and the* **BURGLAR** *are still glaring, nose to nose.*)

They're all worked up – full of passion, heat…At last. we can have the kind of action scenario you've always wanted – a fight to the finish!

MR. GRIFFIN. *(this is a new thought)* Fight?

CONNELLY. *(uneasily, backing away from the* **BURGLAR***)* Fight?

MRS. GRIFFIN. *(happily)* It's really a marvelous idea – two brutish, swinish peasants locked in combat over my –

MR. GRIFFIN. Survival of the fittest…

MRS. GRIFFIN. Exactly!

MR. GRIFFIN. *(beginning to nod)* I like it.

MRS. GRIFFIN. You're not just saying that?

MR. GRIFFIN. *(nodding with growing satisfaction at the increasingly uneasy-looking* **CONNELLY** *and* **BURGLAR***)* The two of them hitting and kicking each other – knocking each other around – I'd enjoy that…

MRS. GRIFFIN. Of course you would!

CONNELLY. *(anxiously)* Uh – excuse me –

MRS. GRIFFIN. It's a real release.

CONNELLY. I don't –

MR. GRIFFIN. What about the ravishing part?

MRS. GRIFFIN. Well, as soon as they finish their savage, bloody battle over me…

(**CONNELLY** *and the* **BURGLAR** *exchange glances.*)

The victor will, of course, lay claim to my soft, white –

CONNELLY. *(hastily)* Hold on – I'd like to oblige, but I'm afraid the fight scene is –

BURGLAR. I've got a bad back and the doctor says –

CONNELLY. It's my knee, you see, I've got this delicate –

MR. GRIFFIN. Quiet! *(glares sternly at them)* This is the last chance for both of you! I want to see a fight and I want to see some ravishing or – *(points gun at* **BURGLAR***)* it's prison for *you* – *(points gun at* **CONNELLY***)* and exposure for *you!...Do I make myself clear?*

(They stare at him numbly.)

Alright! *(to* **MRS. GRIFFIN***)* Where do you want them?

MRS. GRIFFIN. Behind the drapes, I think.

MR. GRIFFIN. *(waving the gun at them)* You heard her!

MRS. GRIFFIN. *(shepherding the dazed* **BURGLAR** *and* **CONNELLY** *towards the drapes)* I think we'll stick with the chateau scenario – its so adaptable… *(happily tucking* **CONNELLY** *behind a drape)* You will be Jacques, as usual, Mr. Connelly… *(turning to the* **BURGLAR***)* And since swineherds don't turn you on… *(draws the* **BURGLAR** *behind another drape as* **MR. GRIFFIN** *marches back to his closet)* you can be a shambling, low-browed stableboy…

MR. GRIFFIN. No malingering! *(closes door on himself)*

MRS. GRIFFIN. *(tucking the* **BURGLAR** *behind a drape)* Places, everybody! *(She takes up her position at the vanity.)* Curtain… *(starts brushing, jiggling)* I do wish my husband, the Marquis, was here with me in my boudoir as I prepare for bed…alone in the chateau except for Jacques the swineherd and that hairy brute of a new stableboy. It makes me shiver, the way they look at me… *(agitated brushing)* And there seems to be bad blood between them – they spit every time they pass each other… *(shudders)* There is such violence in these peasants…I do wish my husband was – Sacre bleu! *(starts, turns fearfully towards drapes)* What is that sound?

MRS. GRIFFIN. Can it be the sound of heavy breathing? *(with emphasis)* The *heavy breathing of two men?*

(We hear nervous panting from behind the drapes.)

Ma foi! I believe it is… *(stands and stares, white-faced at the drapes)* It is coming from behind those drapes… They appear to be moving…Is it just the wind from the open French windows or *(starts)* Caramba! – I mean Mon Dieu! The hulking figures of two men are crouched behind those drapes – I am paralyzed with fright as they tear them aside and advance towards me…advance towards me…advance –

MR. GRIFFIN. *(from his closet)* Do it!

*(***CONNELLY*** and the ***BURGLAR***, panting nervously, emerge from behind the drapes.)*

MRS. GRIFFIN. My heart pounds as they come for me with lust in their tiny, red-rimmed – but wait! They stop – they turn towards each other – their eyes burn with hate…

(The nervously panting twosome eye each other unhappily.)

MR. GRIFFIN. *(from closet)* More hate!

(They try to oblige.)

MRS. GRIFFIN. Their lips draw back from their yellow fangs…

(They expose their teeth.)

like two mongrels snarling over a bone as they crouch, ears flattened to their heads, preparing to spring at each other's throats…

*(The snarling ***CONNELLY*** motions the ***BURGLAR*** to move downstage with him.)*

MR. GRIFFIN. Fight! Kick! Bite!

CONNELLY. *(to the ***BURGLAR***, sotto voce)* We'll fake it – you can win –

BURGLAR. No, no – you can –

MR. GRIFFIN. *(from closet)* No faking – or it's license plates!

MRS. GRIFFIN. *(normal voice)* And Peeping Tom exposure. The question is –

(as they stare desperately at each other)

which of you wants to survive the most?

BURGLAR. *(trapped expression)* Oh, Christ –

*(Launches himself at **CONNELLY**, and they stagger about awkwardly, trying to wrestle each other to the floor.)*

MRS. GRIFFIN. *(back in character, terrified)* Mon Dieu! They are fighting like the crazed animals they are…tearing at each other…showing no mercy…

*(**CONNELLY** and the **BURGLAR** fall onto the bed, where they more or less roll around together.)*

Such brutality…such savagery… *(her eyes glued to the action)* I cannot bear to watch it…

MR. GRIFFIN. *(from the closet)* Hit! Kick! Gouge!

MRS. GRIFFIN. Rending…tearing…

BURGLAR. *(pulling away from **CONNELLY** with sudden, angry emotion)* The *hell* with it! *(struggling up from bed)* What the hell are we fighting' for? There's not going to be any winner – *(points at **MRS. GRIFFIN** and closet 2)* except *them*, don't you understand? They're just using us, playing with us. You know what the so-called winner gets? *(grabs up the bullwhip from beneath the pillow)* This! *(shakes the whip beneath the dazed **CONNELLY**'s nose)* The shaft – just like always – *(Points the whip at **MRS. & MR. GRIFFIN**, who has opened the closet door.)* because they're always holding the whip-hand! Christ, we shouldn't be fighting each other – we should be fighting *them*! I never used to listen to those guys in the jail, but they were right – It's time to rise up against fat cat exploitation! *(holds the whip aloft in a clenched fist, confronting the wide-eyed **MRS. GRIFFIN**)* You're not cracking any more whips – we are! *(cracks the whip over her head)* How do you like it? *(cracks whip again)* And that? *(cracks again)* And that?

MRS. GRIFFIN. *(in a happily dazed whisper) Take* me – *(falls on her back on the bed as* **CONNELLY** *hastily rolls out of the way)* I'm *yours!*

BURGLAR. *(slight pause, staring feverishly at her)* Why not? *(flings whip aside)* All the years you've been screwing us – *(starts for her, tearing off his shirt)* Why shouldn't we screw *you* for a change!

MR. GRIFFIN. *(charging out of the closet)* Get back – *(backs the* **BURGLAR** *off with the gun)* Back!

MRS. GRIFFIN. *(from bed)* But, Charles – he's become just what we've been looking for…passionate…brutal…

MR. GRIFFIN. I am *not* having you ravished by a *Socialist!*

(As they all stare at each other in momentary impasse, a thin, upset woman slightly younger than **MRS. GRIFFIN** *–* **LOUISE** *– pokes her head into the living room.)*

LOUISE. Olivia?

*(***MRS. GRIFFIN*** starts.)*

Are you there?

MRS. GRIFFIN. *(sitting up in sudden panic)* Oh, dear –

MR. GRIFFIN. *(temporarily paralyzed)* Your sister –

LOUISE. *(advancing into the room)* The door was ajar…I've…

(As she looks about distractedly for **MRS. GRIFFIN**, *the* **GRIFFINS** *spring into frenzied action in the bedroom, using the gun and pushing-pulling tactics to hide* **CONNELLY** *behind one drape, the* **BURGLAR** *behind the other.)*

got to see you…

(As **LOUISE** *advances towards the bedroom its half-closed door blocks her view –* **MR. GRIFFIN** *plunges for his closet – and just manages to shut the door on himself as* **LOUISE** *enters the bedroom and stares at* **MRS. GRIFFIN** *in her purple passion lingerie.)*

MRS. GRIFFIN. *(trying to look as casual as possible)* Why, Louise!

LOUISE. *(advancing towards her)* Olivia –

MRS. GRIFFIN. What on earth are you –

LOUISE. *(stopping in front of her)* Olivia – Harrison has left me for a teenager – *(Her face screws up.)* I'm so unhappy...

(She collapses on the bed and begins sobbing bitterly. **MRS. GRIFFIN** *looks at her helplessly, as though she really didn't need this right now, and glances nervously at the drapes.)*

MRS. GRIFFIN. Easy...Take it easy...Try to get a grip on yourself...

LOUISE. *(between sobs)* I can't...

MRS. GRIFFIN. Of course, you can.... Try to sit up...Come on... *(helps her to a sitting position on the bed)* There, that's better. Now...see if you can stand... *(helps the shaky* **LOUISE** *to her feet)* Fine...That's fine...Now just take one step at a time... *(gently guides* **LOUISE** *towards the bedroom door)* That's the way...

LOUISE. *(between sniffles)* Where are we going?

MRS. GRIFFIN. *(with gentle compassion as she guides her out of the bedroom)* You're going home, so you can phone me up and tell me all about it.

LOUISE. *(stopping)* Why do I have to phone you? I'm already here.

MRS. GRIFFIN. Oh. *(unable to deny the logic of this)* Well –

LOUISE. *(pulling away from her)* And I don't want to go home to an empty house! *(moving about with a distraught expression)* I couldn't stand it any longer I got on a train and came into the city. I've just been wandering around, trying to – *(stops and stares at* **MRS. GRIFFIN***)* What's that get-up you're wearing?

MRS. GRIFFIN. Get-up? *(looks down at herself)* Oh. It's just –

LOUISE. You look like a French whore.

MRS. GRIFFIN. Well, actually, it's sort of a show that –

LOUISE. *(wandering distractedly into the bedroom, towards the drapes)* That's what *she* is, you know – a cheap, conniving, gum-chewing little –

MRS. GRIFFIN. *(grabbing her as she is about to walk into the drapes)* Calm yourself! Now...tell me... *(steering her away from the drapes)* how did Harrison get involved with this gum-chewer?

LOUISE. Jogging.

MRS. GRIFFIN. *(unbelievingly)* Jogging?

LOUISE. I thought it was better than sitting. That's all he'd been doing – sitting and moaning…I know whether it was the children leaving for college…or his forty-seventh birthday…or the recession – being a stockbroker, he takes it personally…Anyway, he began sitting around the house all day, moaning about how his life had no meaning and eating peanut butter sandwiches.

MRS. GRIFFIN. How depressing.

LOUISE. It was driving me up the wall. And then… *(Her expression brightens somewhat.)* we discovered BF and for a while it seemed –

MRS. GRIFFIN. BF?

LOUISE. *Biofeedback.* The Scarsdale BF Center features their most advanced mind-body control techniques and – oh, Olivia – *(glowing in a sudden mood shift)* If only you could experience – if only I could express to you what it's done for me…For the first time in my life – *(stands up with shining eyes)* I can make my brain go alpha whenever I want it to! Through BF, I have achieved a kind of inner peace that I never dreamed –

MRS. GRIFFIN. *(a bit impatiently)* What about Harrison?

LOUISE. Harrison? *Oh* my *God* – *(Her face screws up again.)* He… *(sways)* He –

MRS. GRIFFIN. *(grabbing her by the shoulders)* Grip!

LOUISE. I'm gripping! *(getting a tremulous hold on her emotions)* Where…where was I?

MRS. GRIFFIN. *(cautiously letting go of her)* Discovering BF.

LOUISE. Yes! *(suddenly lighting up again)* Oh, Yes! *(She looks out, remembering.)* After we were attached to our Autogenic feedback myographs, things were really good between us for a while. I've never felt closer to Harrison than when we were wired up side by side three times a week…until last month…*(falters)* he suddenly ripped off his wires and announced there was more to life than going alpha…Shortly after that, he took up jogging…*(increasingly grim expression)* He used to jog past her house – she's the daughter of a neighbor…They started meeting every morning when she was walking the family basset hound…Then it was afternoons, too…And then, yesterday… *(ashen-faced)* the basset hound was found tied to a parking meter outside a Hertz Rent-a-car…Scotch-taped to its collar were two notes – one to her parents…and one to – *(sudden anguished remorse)* I should have jogged with him! Why didn't I jog with him!

MRS. GRIFFIN. Don't torture yourself.

LOUISE. The thing that galls me is – I used to buy all her Girl Scout Cookies…*(turns her distraught, tear-stained face to* **MRS. GRIFFIN***)* What am I going to do, Olivia? I feel so humiliated, so abandoned, so –

(suddenly starts and stares at the drape behind which **CONNELLY** *is concealed and which moves slightly as he shifts position)*

What's that?

MRS. GRIFFIN. What?

LOUISE. The drapery. It moved.

MRS. GRIFFIN. It's just the breeze from the open –

LOUISE. There's someone behind there.

MRS. GRIFFIN. I can assure you there is no one behind –

*(***LOUISE** *suddenly pulls the drape aside, revealing* **CONNELLY.** **MRS. GRIFFIN** *stares at him blankly.)*

MRS. GRIFFIN. Oh – Mr. Connelly… *(to* **LOUISE,** *who is backing way)* I'd forgotten about him.

LOUISE. *Forgotten* about –

MRS. GRIFFIN. He's here to…fix the drapery runner – it's been sticking – how's it coming along, Mr. Connelly?

CONNELLY. *(at a loss)* Uh…well. *(fumbling for notebook and pencil)* I've been making observations and –

LOUISE. *(pointing at the other drape)* There's a shoe sticking out from the other one…

MRS. GRIFFIN. *(unhappily)* Shoe?

LOUISE. A man's shoe.

MRS. GRIFFIN. It's probably one of Charles'. He's always –

LOUISE. There's a foot in it – *(jerks the drape aside, revealing the* **BURGLAR***)* Just what is going –

(The **BURGLAR** *makes a break for the bathroom and fire escape, causing* **MR. GRIFFIN** *to come charging out of closet 2 in his high-heeled shoes brandishing the gun.)*

MR. GRIFFIN. Freeze – or I'll drop you in your tracks.

(The **BURGLAR** *freezes.* **LOUISE** *stares at* **MR. GRIFFIN** *in his cocktail dress, then at the others.)*

LOUISE. *Oh* my *God –* *(backs away from them all with an increasingly distraught expression)* You're having an orgy…

MRS. GRIFFIN. Now there's nothing to be alarmed –

LOUISE. Keep away from me!

MRS. GRIFFIN. But I'm your sister…

LOUISE. I was depending on you to… *(blinking back her tears)* help me…give me some guidance…

MRS. GRIFFIN. And we will!

LOUISE. How? *(takes them all in dolefully)* You're in worse shape than I am…

MRS. GRIFFIN. *(frowning)* Actually, we're all benefiting from a –

LOUISE. Who are these people and – *(pointing tearfully at* **MR. GRIFFIN***)* Why is he wearing a dress?

MRS. GRIFFIN. That's all part of the therapy.

LOUISE. What therapy?

*(***MR. GRIFFIN** *herds the* **BURGLAR** *back across the room with the gun.)*

MRS. GRIFFIN. We've all been benefiting from a wonderful new form of group therapy, pioneered by Dr. Leopold Baumgartner. As a matter of fact – *(eyes* **LOUISE***; then, excitedly) yes* – I think we could even benefit your case.

LOUISE. What do you –

MR. GRIFFIN. Now hold on – things are crowded enough as it is!

MRS. GRIFFIN. Would you ask me to deny my own sister in her time of need?

MR. GRIFFIN. I –

MRS. GRIFFIN. Look at her!

(They all look at the hollow-eyed **LOUISE.***)*

Can't you see? This is a woman who has reached rock bottom…a woman who has been rejected…abandoned…humiliated beyond belief…

*(***LOUISE***'s expression becomes, if possible, even more morose.)*

What has she got to look forward to but empty days and lonely nights…the whispers and secret smiles of her neighbors…or – worse still – *(in hushed tones, caught up by the tragic pathos of it all)* the pitying expression in their averted eyes as she passes….

*(***LOUISE*** begins to sway as her eyes fill with hopeless tears.)*

until one night, driven by black despair…she gets up out of her lonely bed and goes to the bathroom and stretching out her hand for the last time…reaches for that bottle of sleeping –

LOUISE. *(faintly)* Oh my God…

(She starts to collapse in a half-swoon – **MRS. GRIFFIN** *props her up with difficulty as she moans.)*

I don't want to die…

MRS. GRIFFIN. *(struggling to hold* **LOUISE** *up)* Is that what you want on your conscience, Charles?

MR. GRIFFIN. *(uneasily)* I didn't do it.

LOUISE. Nobody wants me…

(as **MRS. GRIFFIN** *staggers about under her dead weight)*

I'm a *mess…*

MRS. GRIFFIN. You are not! Is she, Charles?

(MR. GRIFFIN *looks unconvinced.*)

Mr. Connelly?

CONNELLY. *(uncomfortably)* Well…I've seen worse – I mean –

LOUISE. A useless, dried-up, ugly –

MRS. GRIFFIN. You don't have to be… *(trying unsuccessfully to get* LOUISE *upright)* You can be vibrant and sexy and – *(breaks off)* Will someone *help* me?

(MR. GRIFFIN *waves the gun at* CONNELLY, *who goes over and gingerly helps prop up the sagging* LOUISE.)

Locked up inside of you, Louise, is a warm, desirable woman…

LOUISE. *(sagging between them)* No…

MRS. GRIFFIN. Yes…A woman who stands out at cocktail parties…who glows with an aura of sexual musk that men find strangely attractive –

LOUISE. *(shaking her head sadly)* No…

MRS. GRIFFIN. *Yes*…A woman who, if she wanted to, could have Harrison crawling back to her on his hands and knees…

(LOUISE *stops shaking her head.*)

begging for forgiveness…

LOUISE. *(after a long pause, still sagging)* You…really think she's there?

(MRS. GRIFFIN *nods.*)

Then why won't she come out?

MRS. GRIFFIN. She *will,* but you have to *fight* to free her!

(*as she and* CONNELLY *struggle to stand* LOUISE *completely upright*)

You have to face your fears and exorcise your demons – convince yourself that you're not a loser but a winner!

(*They cautiously let go of* LOUISE. *She sways slightly, but remains erect.*)

LOUISE. How…how do I do that?

MRS. GRIFFIN. *(with a fervent glow)* Through Dr. Baumgartner's revolutionary "Live Your Fantasy" therapy!

LOUISE. Live Your –

MR. GRIFFIN. Damn it all – what about *our* therapy!

MRS. GRIFFIN. *(turning her glowing eyes on him)* But this should be even more stimulating, dear – after all, we're enriching the basic scenario…

MR. GRIFFIN. *(suspiciously)* How?

MRS. GRIFFIN. *(enthusiastically indicating* **LOUISE***)* We're *both* going to be ravished!

LOUISE. *(uneasily)* Ravished?

MRS. GRIFFIN. It's all part of the therapy, nothing to worry about. Now! *(briskly, getting things organized)* What we're going to do is reproduce the basic humiliation sequence – Harrison lying to you, betraying you, being seduced by a teenager et cetera, et cetera, only – *(turning to* **LOUISE***)* this time we add a confrontation scene so you can get in *your* licks! *(beams at her sister)* How do you like it so far?

LOUISE. I…I'm not sure I –

MRS. GRIFFIN. Haven't you had any fantasies about – you know – finding them together…confronting them with your rage and passion…

LOUISE. *(after a pause)* Yes…only – they always end up laughing at me…

MRS. GRIFFIN. Well, they won't be laughing this time, and you know why? Because you won't be confronting them as a weepy loser. *(Moves about, caught up in the vision, which she manages to make her own.)* You'll be cool, faintly scornful…a woman whose faint, mysterious aura of musk reaches out to Harrison and pulls at him, causing the little vein in his forehead to start throbbing with –

LOUISE. Just a minute! *(uncertainly)* You expect me to…act out my private life and emotions in front of strangers?

MRS. GRIFFIN. But that's the whole point of group therapy – you can be more uninhibited in front of strangers...*(indicating the* **BURGLAR** *and* **CONNELLY***)* We *never* socialize outside the group. *(as* **LOUISE** *still looks uncertain)* It's really an advanced form of biofeedback.

LOUISE. Bio –

MRS. GRIFFIN. Instead of plugging into a machine, we plug into each other!

LOUISE. I...I don't know.

MRS. GRIFFIN. You don't want to stay like *this*, do you?

LOUISE. No...

MRS. GRIFFIN. Then – *(with earnest conviction)* give it *everything* you've *got!* Now then! *(organizing again)* You will, of course, play yourself and...yes... *(eyeing* **CONNELLY** *speculatively)* You'll do nicely in the role of Harrison, Mr. Connelly. You both have a weight problem.

CONNELLY. *(not liking the sound of this)* Jesus...

MRS. GRIFFIN. I'll be the teenager while Charles will give us moral support from the closet. Now the basic plot as I –

MR. GRIFFIN. *(indicating the sullen* **BURGLAR***)* What about him? I want to keep my eye on him.

MRS. GRIFFIN. *(frowning at the* **BURGLAR***)* I really don't see how I can fit him into – wait a minute – *(Her expression clears.)* Of course! He can be the basset hound!

BURGLAR. Now hold on –

MR. GRIFFIN. A dog – I like that.

BURGLAR. I'm not –

MR. GRIFFIN. Oh, yes, you are! *(points gun at him)* Get down there and be a dog... *(gestures grimly with gun) Down,* boy!

(Muttering to himself, the **BURGLAR** *drops down on all fours.)*

MRS. GRIFFIN. *(happily)* Well! It's really starting to shape up...Now remember, Mr. Connelly, you are no longer a brutish, thick-necked peasant on the eve of the French

Revolution… *(briskly, to the morose-looking* **CONNELLY***)* You are now a paunchy, thick-necked stock broker from Scarsdale, whom we discover jogging down a lonely road –

CONNELLY. *(uneasily)* Jogging?

MRS. GRIFFIN. As a matter of fact, why don't you start now – it would help get us all in the mood.

CONNELLY. Listen, I'm really not in shape for –

MR. GRIFFIN. *(pointing gun at him)* Jog!

*(***CONNELLY*** begins half-hearted in-the-place jogging as the* **BURGLAR** *watches from all fours with a certain dour canine satisfaction)*

MRS. GRIFFIN. Very good! *(to* **LOUISE***)* We'll be improvising as we go along, but here is the basic outline: I, of course, am a lovely, young teenager…

*(***LOUISE*** does not appear overjoyed to hear this.)*

I am walking my basset hound – *(indicating the* **BURGLAR***)* with my hair stirring softly in the breeze… when Harrison comes jogging along and stares with pent-up yearning at the radiant vision of youth and freshness that I present.

*(***LOUISE*** looks increasingly unhappy.)*

When Harrison succumbs immediately to the more obvious charms of my soft, white, vulnerable body, *you* appear on the scene and manage to win him back with your subtler, less-visible-to-the-eye –

LOUISE. *(firmly)* I want to play the teenager.

MRS. GRIFFIN. *(frowning)* I don't see how –

LOUISE. You always give yourself the good parts!

MRS. GRIFFIN. But, Louise –

CONNELLY. *(wheezing as he jogs)* Can I stop now?

MR. GRIFFIN. *Jog!*

MRS. GRIFFIN. *(to* **LOUISE***)* You've got to play yourself – it's all for your benefit…and after all, you *are* going to win out in the end.

(**LOUISE** *doesn't appear too sure of this as* **MRS. GRIFFIN** *turns away.*)

MRS. GRIFFIN. Alright, group – let's try for a real break-through. *Places*

(**MR. GRIFFIN** *marches in his military fashion to the closet as* **MRS. GRIFFIN** *positions herself next to the canine* **BURGLAR.**)

Remember, Louise – try to look upon Mr. Connelly as Harrison.

LOUISE. *(eyeing the wheezing, still-jogging* **CONNELLY***)* I'll try.

MRS. GRIFFIN. Now when you see me – the teenager – seduc-ing your husband and when you see him responding helplessly to my –

LOUISE. *(bleakly)* Obvious charms.

MRS. GRIFFIN. Yes. It will stir up powerful emotions in you – and that's *good* – that means the therapy is really working – let it happen…

LOUISE. *(tensely)* All right.

MRS. GRIFFIN. When you can't stand our intimacy any longer – when you feel like challenging me – do it – let your long-repressed sensuality go on the scene, spraying musk in all directions, inflaming Harrison's passion to the point where he picks you up in his arms –

CONNELLY. Jesus…

MRS. GRIFFIN. – and carries you off to –

MR. GRIFFIN. *(at closet)* Hold on! *(as* **MRS. GRIFFIN** *turns to him)* Who's* going to ravish *you?*

MRS. GRIFFIN. *(slight frown)* Oh, that's right… *(looks down at the* **BURGLAR***, shrugs)* I guess we'll have to try *him* again.

BURGLAR. *(snappishly)* I'm supposed to be a dog.

MR. GRIFFIN. You are *not* going to be ravished by this Socialist cur! *(indicates* **CONNELLY***)* After Connelly does *her* he's going to do *you* and that's the way it's going to be!

CONNELLY. *(stopping dead in his tracks)* Oh, Christ...

MRS. GRIFFIN. Places, everybody!

(**MR. GRIFFIN** *steps into the closet, turns around, points gun at* **BURGLAR.***)*

MR. GRIFFIN. Keep your *nose* to the *ground.*

(He closes the door on himself and disappears from sight.)

MRS. GRIFFIN. All right – we're starting... *(to* **LOUISE***)* Don't be nervous. Just let it happen.

(**LOUISE** *nods tensely, and* **MRS. GRIFFIN** *turns to the panting, wheezing* **CONNELLY.***)*

Harrison?

(He continues to pant.)

Harrison!

CONNELLY. *(becoming aware that she means him)* Huh?

MRS. GRIFFIN. Start jogging, please.

CONNELLY. Oh...Can't I just –

MR. GRIFFIN. *(from closet)* Do it!

(**CONNELLY** *starts jogging again.* **MRS. GRIFFIN** *gets a wide-eyed teen-aged look and pats the* **BURGLAR** *on his head.)*

MRS. GRIFFIN. Come on, boy!

(The **BURGLAR** *gives her a dirty look.)*

It's such a nice day...Why don't we go for a walk....

(She moves in the direction of **CONNELLY** *with the* **BURGLAR** *morosely pad-padding along at her side.)*

All the little buds are opening and the birds and the bees – oh, look! *(as though spotting the unhappily-jogging* **CONNELLY** *for the first time)* There's that nice Mr. Abernathy... *(sotto-voce to* **CONNELLY** *in her normal voice)* That's your last name.

CONNELLY. *(wheezing)* Oh.

MRS. GRIFFIN. *(back in character, waving at him)* Hi, Mr. Abernathy!

CONNELLY. *(gasping for breath)* Uh…hullo.

MRS. GRIFFIN. It's such a beautiful day, isn't it? I mean, to be outdoors with the sap running and everything…

CONNELLY. *(increasingly out of breath)* I…I… *(abruptly stops in his tracks)* Look, I can't jog and talk at the same time,

MRS. GRIFFIN. *(sotto-voce, normal voice)* All right; only stay in character. *(teenager voice)* Don't you *feel* it, Mr. Abernathy?

CONNELLY. *(not really interested, still gasping to get his breath back)* Sap…Yeah…Sap…

MRS. GRIFFIN. *(sotto-voce)* Say something complimentary…

CONNELLY. *(floundering)* Uh…. that's a nice dog you've got there…

MRS. GRIFFIN. *(as the **BURGLAR** looks daggers at **CONNELLY**)* Why thank you! He's a basset hound!

CONNELLY. *(awkwardly)* You don't say.

MRS. GRIFFIN. *(sotto-voce)* Don't stop.

CONNELLY. *(at a loss)* Uh…

MRS. GRIFFIN. *(sotto-voce)* Keep it going.

CONNELLY. *(not really knowing what he's saying)* We…we had a dog once name of Gertrude, a dachshund, only we had to get rid of her because she was always yapping and kept piddling all over the –

MR. GRIFFIN. *(from closet)* Get *off* the *dog*!

MRS. GRIFFIN. *(sotto-voce)* Say something about *me*.

CONNELLY. Uh… *(stares at her, looking for something to say that won't offend)* That's quite an outfit you got on – I mean, for being outdoors like we are…

MRS. GRIFFIN. *(back in character)* Thank you! I suppose it *is* a bit skimpy, but…*(confessing shyly)* I seem to be so hot-blooded that I don't need much covering over body, even outdoors. *(takes a step closer to him)* You don't have to take my word for it…Touch me…

*(**CONNELLY** stares at her.)*

Go ahead, Harrison – you don't mind if I call you Harrison, do you?

(**LOUISE** *looks grim.*)

Touch me!

(**CONNELLY** *gingerly reaches out to touch her and she takes his hand.*)

My, your hand is warm! *(looks up at him, wide-eyed)* You must be hot-blooded, too...

CONNELLY. *(out of his depth)* I...

MRS. GRIFFIN. It's as though the sap is running through both our veins...at the same time...Oh, Harrison... *(takes a step closer)* You think I don't know why you've taken up jogging? It's to get away from your wife, isn't it?

CONNELLY. *(as* **LOUISE** *looks even grimmer)* Uh –

MRS. GRIFFIN. I know you find me strangely attractive...I know you've been watching me from the apple tree outside my window when I am naked in my bath . .

CONNELLY. I...I was making observations on –

MRS. GRIFFIN. No need to deny it.... Oh, Harrison...*(takes a step closer)* How can I blame you for desiring my youthful freshness, which still has the bloom of innocence upon it...How you must torture yourself, night after night, thinking of me as you lie there beside your sexually repressed wife...But, Harrison –

(**LOUISE** *looks completely beside herself as* **MRS. GRIFFIN** *leans seductively against the nervous-looking* **CONNELLY**.)

It's a crime against nature to deny what we feel for each other. We must be true to the yearnings deep within us, the tug of –

(**LOUISE** *charges into the scene and wrenches them apart.*)

LOUISE. Get your hands off him!

MRS. GRIFFIN. Why – Mrs. Abernathy –

LOUISE. *(glaring at* **CONNELLY***)* You're supposed to be jogging – *(thrusts her face into his) Jog!*

(The startled **CONNELLY** *starts jogging again with surprising energy.)*

MRS. GRIFFIN. *(still in teenager role)* Now Mrs. Abernathy, you –

LOUISE. You can drop the little girl act. You think I don't know what you're up to?

MRS. GRIFFIN. *(normal-voiced)* We're simply trying to help –

LOUISE. Bullshit! If it hadn't been the teenager, it probably *would* have been you! You think I never saw you flirting with Harrison every time we invited you for dinner?

MRS. GRIFFIN. I never –

LOUISE. Come off it! *(Trembles with anger as* **MR. GRIFFIN***'s head, with a rather impatient expression, peers out of his closet.)* You think I've forgotten how you tried to steal Billy Woodson from me?

MRS. GRIFFIN. Why would I want to steal a boy with spots all over –

LOUISE. To put me down! And I'm sick of it! *(feverishly)* Just because Nature gave you bigger... *(gestures distractedly at* **MRS. GRIFFIN***'s figure) boobs* than me –

MRS. GRIFFIN. *(frostily)* That has nothing to do with –

LOUISE. All you big boobers think you can lord it over the rest of us – well – let me tell you something – *(thumps herself on the chest with feverish defiance)* I've got just as much musk as you do!

MR. GRIFFIN. *(to the still-jogging* **CONNELLY***)* Pssst – that's your cue!

CONNELLY. Huh?

MR. GRIFFIN. *Ravish,* man, *ravish!*

CONNELLY. Uh... *(nervously eyeing* **MRS. GRIFFIN** *and* **LOUISE***, who glare at each other with sibling anger)* I forget who's first...

LOUISE. *(turning her glare to him)* First for what?

CONNELLY. *(conciliatory tone)* Ravishing...

LOUISE. *(advancing on him)* If there's any *ravishing* to be done – *(thrusts her face into his, causing the alarmed* **CONNELLY** *to fall backward on the bed)* I'll do it!

MRS. GRIFFIN. *(shocked)* Louise!

MR. GRIFFIN. *(emerging from his closet)* This is anarchy…

LOUISE. It's the turn of the worm! *(strides about excitedly)* It's freedom now.

MRS. GRIFFIN. Calm your –

LOUISE. No more calm! No more passive little Goody Two-shoes! All my life, I've let other people make choices for me – *(stops in front of the stern-looking* **MR. GRIFFIN**) people like you, you male chauvinist pervert!

MR. GRIFFIN. You're disrupting an important –

LOUISE. *(thrusting her face into his)* Bug off. And – *(grabs the gun from the startled* **MR. GRIFFIN***'s hand) give* me that! *(moves about feverishly)*

MR. GRIFFIN. *(nervously)* Be careful with that –

LOUISE. No more careful! *(eyes the gun with fierce joy)* This is *power!* I've never *had* power before! I *like* it!

MRS. GRIFFIN. *(soothingly)* Louise, can't we –

LOUISE. No, we can't! I know what you want –

(advances on **MRS. GRIFFIN**, *who backs away)*

You want me to go back to thinking pink and keeping my knees together and baking brownies while you're having orgies and my children are smoking pot and my husband is running off with teenagers…

MRS. GRIFFIN. I never –

LOUISE. Oh, yes, you did! You and everybody else have always made me feel I wasn't much and the best I could hope for were the small rewards of virtue – well, you're not going to have good old Louise to kick around any more! She's going to *sizzle* and *smoke* and have some *adventure* in her life – *(glares at* **CONNELLY** *who has struggled to a sitting position on the bed)* and that doesn't mean an overweight stockbroker who bites his nails and moans in his sleep – do I make myself clear?

CONNELLY. *(hastily)* No problem…

LOUISE. *(moving about restlessly)* I spent twenty boring years with him because everybody said what a good match it was for someone like me… *(angrily)* I'm not even attracted to his body type! Well, now I'm going to find something that turns me on…something lean and hungry with haunted, vulnerable…

*(She stops at the figure of the **BURGLAR**, who has been surreptitiously crawling on all fours towards the bathroom fire escape, and who freezes as **LOUISE** looks down at him with the gun more or less pointed in his direction.)*

eyes…

*(There is a pause as they look at each other; the **BURGLAR**'s expression is decidedly haunted and vulnerable. **LOUISE** takes him in as though she's never really looked at him before, then murmurs shyly.)*

Hello.

BURGLAR. *(uneasily)* Hi.

LOUISE. *(after another pause)* What are you doing down there?

BURGLAR. Being a dog.

LOUISE. *(angrily, to her sister)* Who are you to turn people into dogs!

MRS. GRIFFIN. He's a burglar.

MR. GRIFFIN. A common criminal.

LOUISE. *Oh,* my *God. (stares, wide-eyed, down at the **BURGLAR**)* Is it true?

BURGLAR. Well…I wouldn't go so far as to –

LOUISE. Get up! *(eyes him with growing fascination as he gets stiffly to his feet)* How you must have suffered…

BURGLAR. *(with feeling)* You said it, lady. For the last –

LOUISE. Call me Louise.

BURGLAR. All right.

LOUISE. What's your name?

BURGLAR. Uh…*(Any name will do.)* Joe.

MR. GRIFFIN. Can't we dispense with this –

LOUISE. *(pointing the gun at him) Don't interrupt.*

> *(**MR. GRIFFIN** subsides and **LOUISE** continues, bitterly eyeing the **GRIFFINS**.)*

They drove you to a life of crime, didn't they, Joe – with their constant put-downs, always taking, never giving…

BURGLAR. Well… *(This sounds good to him.)* Yeah.

LOUISE. A life of tremendous risks and… *(turning to him)* constant danger and *(increasingly warm expression)* hairbreadth escapes and –

BURGLAR. Getting caught…

LOUISE. And aching loneliness…*(steps close to him and confesses tremulously)* They've made me suffer, too.

BURGLAR. *(keeping one eye on the gun)* No kidding.

LOUISE. I want to help you, Joe.

BURGLAR. *(dazedly, as the **GRIFFINS** exchange uneasy glances)* You do? *(sudden, wild hope)* To get *out* of here?

LOUISE. And *more – together.* They've taken from us now it's *our* turn!

BURGLAR. Well – *(seeing she really means it)* All right! Let's *do* it!

MRS. GRIFFIN. Just a minute! *(moving towards **LOUISE**)* Louise, aren't you really carrying things a little too –

BURGLAR. *(to **LOUISE**)* Would you do me a little favor?

LOUISE. Of course.

BURGLAR. Make them crawl.

LOUISE. A pleasure. *(points her gun at the **GRIFFINS**)* Crawl.

MR. GRIFFIN. Do you expect me to believe you'd shoot your own flesh and –

LOUISE. *(feverishly, waving gun)* I'm very unpredictable right now because – *(The gun discharges, startling **LOUISE** as much as anybody.)* You see? It's because I'm undergoing metamorphosis and my emotions are bubbling over – *crawl!*

> *(The **GRIFFINS** drop to their hands and knees.)*

MR. GRIFFIN. *(sourly, to* **MRS. GRIFFIN** *as he crawls off)* Your sister certainly has enriched things…

MRS. GRIFFIN. *(crawling after him with as much serenity as she can muster)* She's not well, Charles. We must try to have –

BURGLAR. *(going to closet 1)* Don't talk – *crawl.*

LOUISE. I'm so excited! *(glowingly eyes the* **BURGLAR** *at the closet)* We're going to grab big handfuls of life!

BURGLAR. *(coming out with an armful of fur coats)* We'll start with these.

MRS. GRIFFIN. My coats!

LOUISE. Freeze! *(explaining)* He's just robbing from the rich to give to the poor – it's a revolutionary act.

BURGLAR. Hey, that's right – I'm sort of into that now.

LOUISE. *(glowing at him)* We're *both* having our consciousness raised.

BURGLAR. *(pulling her and the coats towards bathroom fire escape)* Let's *do* it!

LOUISE. *(inside bathroom, rapturously) Oh* my *God* – a fire escape…

*(***LOUISE*** rushes happily to* **MRS. GRIFFIN***, hugs her from behind.)*

LOUISE. You were right, Olivia – the therapy really works! *(Rushes to the bathroom, then turns back. Looks out with shining-eyed wonder)* We're going to be Robin Hood and Maid Marion!

(She slams the door closed. **MRS. GRIFFIN** *goes to the door, tugs on it.)*

MRS. GRIFFIN. She's locked it! *(Through the door as* **GRIFFIN** *gets up and comes over.)* Louise? I don't think we've really worked things through for you – I don't think you…Louise?

MR. GRIFFIN. She's gone. So has he. *(turns away from the door)* I can't really say I'm going to miss them.

MRS. GRIFFIN. Well – *(shrugs resignedly)* There's no use crying over spilt…whatever. *(turning to* **CONNELLY***, slumped on the bed)* There's still Mr. Connelly.

(**MR. GRIFFIN** *frowns as* **CONNELLY** *reacts to this by pushing himself off the bed and plodding towards his tool-box.*)

MR. GRIFFIN. Where do you think you're going?

CONNELLY. *(reaching for the toolbox) Home.*

MR. GRIFFIN. You're not shirking your obligations! Have you forgotten those photos –

CONNELLY. Threats don't work anymore, Mr. Griffin, when what's already been done to you seems worse than what *could* be done to you. *(starts to exit, hesitates, turns back)* I'm no washout, you understand, but – *(with feeling)* I've been *whipped* and *jogged* and *Frenchified* and revved up and knocked down and – *I'm quittin' the team!*

(*He stalks off with dignity and exits. The* **GRIFFINS** *stare after him.*)

MR. GRIFFIN. Damn. *(moves to the bed)* Damn. Damn. *(sits gloomily)* The whole day's a waste. I should have gone to the office.

MRS. GRIFFIN. *(reflectively echoing* **CONNELLY***'s exit line)* Team…the team… *(suddenly glowing with a new sense of wondrous revelation)* You know, Charles – I think Mr. Connelly was trying to tell us something…

MR. GRIFFIN. *(unconvinced)* What?

MRS. GRIFFIN. He was trying to tell us that – *(turning excitedly to* **MR. GRIFFIN***)* we've been misinterpreting Dr. Baumgartner!

MR. GRIFFIN. How?

MRS. GRIFFIN. Perhaps he never meant for us to enlist others in our search…even if we felt it was for their health and happiness, too…Perhaps we're supposed to get back to… *(gropingly)* the two of us.

MR. GRIFFIN. You mean…*(dawning awareness, as at a wonderful new thought)* a one-to-one relationship?

MRS. GRIFFIN. *(coming to* **MR. GRIFFIN** *as he rises from the bed)* Simple…natural…direct…

MR. GRIFFIN. *(taking her hands in his)* The way it was at the beginning.

MRS. GRIFFIN. Well – *(removes her hands with a slight frown)* not exactly.

MR. GRIFFIN. Oh?

MRS. GRIFFIN. *(after a pause)* You always had to be in charge. The timing. The positions. The duration.

MR. GRIFFIN. Someone has to be captain of the ship.

MRS. GRIFFIN. A bed isn't a ship. There were lots of times you sailed off happily and I never did get there.

MR. GRIFFIN. Why didn't you –

MRS. GRIFFIN. Say something? I never got the chance! You'd bounce off the mattress feeling great, and be off to a business call or a golf game. You never once…in all the years of our marriage… *(with deep yearning and sincerity)* considered other options in bed.

MR. GRIFFIN. *(helpless shrug)* It's the way I was brought up, I guess.

MRS. GRIFFIN. *(compassionately)* Another victim of macho brain-washing. I think that's the core of the problem, Charles. Something…*deep* inside you is struggling to achieve a new flexibility in your nature…

(He stares at her, then down at himself.)

It's a fight I believe you can win….for *both* our sakes –

MR. GRIFFIN. You're right, Livvy!

(He eyes her with glowing conviction.)

I *feel* it now!

MRS. GRIFFIN. Are you sure?

MR. GRIFFIN. Yes! Oh, yes! *(as they look at each other with an air of tender commitment)* Shall we begin?

MRS. GRIFFIN. I'm ready.

(They turn away from each other. Moment of hesitation. They turn back and look into each other's eyes, silently communicating…something. **MR. GRIFFIN** *then slowly*

turns towards the dressing table, sits down, and starts brushing his hair as **MRS. GRIFFIN** *goes and hides behind the drape.)*

MR. GRIFFIN. As I prepare for bed, alone in my boudoir… *(brush, brush)* there is nobody else in the chateau but *Jacqueline,* the flirtateous, big-boobed daughter of the swineherd… *(agitation from behind the drapes)* I have heard rumors that she is a ravisher of women…and while I try to brush them from my mind… *(brush, brush, increased agitation from the drapes)* I *have* noticed a certain expression in her boldly staring eyes…

(heavy breathing from behind the increasingly agitated drapes)

whenever she catches a glimpse of my soft…white – *(slight frown)* at the same time, athletic and well-built–

*(***MRS. GRIFFIN*** *tears aside the drape and strides toward him with an aroused expression.)*

but extremely vulnerable body.

MRS. GRIFFIN. *(at vanity table)* Up!

(He gets up; she points at the bed.)

Down!

(He sits on the bed.)

On your back.

MR. GRIFFIN. Back?

MRS. GRIFFIN. *Back.*

MR. GRIFFIN. *(slight pause; then with a delightedly aroused expression)* Happy… *(lies down flat)* to oblige.

(curtain)

End of Play

PROPERTY LIST

On Stage Preset: All Doors Closed
Bar Area S.R. Platform
Armchair – D.R.
T.V. on stand D.R. – S.R. of chair
Bar – U.C. flush with wall – D.S. of mirrored shelves
Bar Stool – D.L. of bar on spike marks
Pedestal – U.R. of cubby area – with brush
Mirror – U.R. cubby area on wall
Light switch – in off position (down)
1. Ice Bucket with ice
2. Napkins
3. (2) Glasses
4. Scotch Decanter almost full
5. Work of art
6. Phone (plugged in)

Bed Area D.R. of Center –
Bed D.C.R. preset with 2 pillows, white silk sheets, comforter folded over,
at head of bed, whip under DL3 pillow (check that whip is well hidden).
Telephone table D.S.R. of bed
Telephone table D.S.
1. Phone – – secured – cord tucked under table
2. Lighter – check flame
3. Ashtray – secured – with a little water in bowl
4. Humidor – secured – with 4 cigars that have been moistened; top of
    humidor is put on very lightly.

Vanity Table Area –
Vanity table U.L.
2 Vanity Stools
1pink stool S.R. on right side of vanity
1brown stool D.S. end of vanity
1. Stand-up mirror – secured
2. Hair brush
3. Nail buff
4. Hand mirror
5. Comb
6. Longine (box)

Second level
1. Vogue Magazine
2. Jewelry Box – Hinges S.L. side

Dresser Area –
Dresser U.L.
2 Lamps
Watch-in top drawer (S.R.)
Gun-in top drawer (S.L.) *UNLOADED*
Dressing

Window Area –
Curtains – practical – opened
Radiator – check that knob is screwed on

Closet Area –
Closet #1 (dressing) 4 furs on hangers – S.L. to S.R. 1 coat, 1cape, 1big animal fur, 1 little animal fur – Mrs. G.
Closet #2 (dressing) wallet with money-in black suit coat pocket (D.S. pocket) 1 chair – Mr G

Off S.R. –
Door Slam S.R. wing area

Prop Table S.R. –
1. Tool Box-with hammer-Connelly
2. 1 Photo – Mrs. G.
3. Rabbit's foot – Burglar
4. Lock pick set – Burglar
5. Pack of Kleenex – Burglar
Suitcase on Bar platform behind wall-arrow on U.S. side

Personals –
1. Mrs. G.-Ring
2. Louis+Purse
3. Connelly – Pad and pencil, Wallet

Intermission –
1. Strike suitcase
2. Re-hang furs in Mrs. G. closet
3. Turn off blue fights S.R.
4. Open bathroom doors all the way
5. Check that closets 1& 2 are closed
Load gun with blank

Shopping Infomation –
1. Butane– for lighter
2. Coca cola – for scotch
3. Blanks for gun – Winchester
4. Cigars

COSTUME PLOT

BURGLAR
Grey green tweed sport coat
White long sleeved shirt
Narrow dark tie
Grey green wool trousers
Grey suede rubber soled shoes
Dark socks
Black gloves

MR. CONNELLY
Green blue work shirt – "SUPER" on back
Green blue work trousers
Dark socks
Light brown rubber sole shoes
Black belt

MRS. GRIFFIN
Rigged partial breakaway hostess gown, wrap-around and belted with red skirt, peach brocade gown with lapels that can close up to high neck and open to low décolletée
Black corselet, trimmed with lace, rhinestones, beads etc., with garters and black lace shoulder straps
Dance briefs, trimmed with lace, bikini cut
All sheer panty hose
Black fish net stockings
Black high heeled shoes with rhinestones
One ring

MR. GRIFFIN
Pink silk chiffon with gold glitter overlaid on gold and pink metallic tissue cocktail dress with spaghetti straps
Sandals with medium heels, gold or dyed pink to match dress

LOUISE
Denim blue dress suit with print polyester blouse attached to skirt
Maroon felt hat
Maroon snake skin envelope purse
Black slip
Brown shoes
Panty hose
Brown gloves

There are no changes with the exception of Mrs. Griffin. Her change is on stage and she is under dressed.

www.ingramcontent.com/pod-product-compliance
Lightning Source LLC
Chambersburg PA
CBHW061033050726
47592CB00004B/1425